# "You don't ne~~~ deal with me," Joe said, taking the glass away from her.

"Oh, yes, I do. I wouldn't mind having the rest of the bottle. In fact, I think I need to be totally pie-eyed to deal with you, Officer Gilardini."

He put down his own glass and turned back to her. "Then let's see how you're progressing toward your goal." Rising to his knees, he cupped her elbows and drew her up to face him.

"What are you doing?" Leigh asked.

"Administering a field test for sobriety."

"You're going to see if I can walk a straight line on my knees?"

His mustache twitched in amusement. "If you can do that, drunk or sober, we ought to get you on Letterman." He held up his index finger. "Follow the movement of my finger with your eyes."

She laughed. "I think I need more champagne."

His voice was gentle but firm as he leaned toward her. "No, you don't," he murmured. "You're a Singleton." His mouth hovered above hers. "You can take the heat."

Dear Reader,

The mind of a cop functions differently from those of us not in law enforcement. If I suspected that before, I know it now—thanks to excellent input from police psychologist Dr. Kevin Gilmartin. I also suspect that the mentality he described would apply just as well to Pat Garrett or Wyatt Earp as it does to a modern-day officer of the law. The job description is still the same—catch the bad guys. I find that admirable…and sexy. I had a good time writing about Joe Gilardini, a twenty-year veteran of the NYPD who finds the West is still in need of taming.

Joe could use a little taming himself, and Leigh Singleton is the woman to do it. In writing about Leigh, I allowed myself to consider the possibility of psychic powers, which have always intrigued me. The more I researched, the more I moved into Leigh's world. Crystals hanging in my office window bathe the room in rainbows and New Age music plays on my stereo. I've even experimented with aromatherapy. If all this sounds like more fun than one person is supposed to have, then you'll understand why I've loved doing this series. Thanks for visiting the True Love with me!

Happy trails,

Vicki Lewis Thompson

# Vicki Lewis Thompson
# THE LAWMAN

## Harlequin Books

TORONTO • NEW YORK • LONDON
AMSTERDAM • PARIS • SYDNEY • HAMBURG
STOCKHOLM • ATHENS • TOKYO • MILAN
MADRID • WARSAW • BUDAPEST • AUCKLAND

For John Cheek, an officer and a gentleman

ISBN 0-373-25663-9

THE LAWMAN

# 1

A MAN WAS ABOUT to kiss him.

As the guy's breath began to tickle his mustache, Joe blinked and tried to clear the fog from his brain. "If you try mouth-to-mouth resuscitation, you're a dead man," he mumbled, giving him the benefit of the doubt.

"Never learned it, anyway." The guy—Joe realized it was the business type who had been in the doomed elevator with him—sat back on his heels and loosened his tie with such apparent relief that Joe decided maybe he'd been wrong about the other guy's intentions. But these days, you just didn't know.

"Here." The businessman reached into the inside pocket of his suit coat and handed Joe a handkerchief. "You're bleeding somewhere."

"No joke." Joe could feel it dripping from his chin. He pressed the snowy-white handkerchief, no doubt monogrammed, against the gash. Visibility was poor in the crumpled elevator, which was hot and smelled of dust and fried wires. He'd never liked small spaces. "How's the other guy?"

"I'll survive," said a voice from the back wall.

"Says his back hurts," volunteered the businessman. "I told him not to move."

*What a genius.* "Good," Joe said aloud. "Moving a back-injury case and severing his spinal cord would top this episode off nicely." Still holding the bloody handkerchief to his chin, he struggled to a sitting position, wincing at the sharp pain in his left forearm. Probably broken. Great. Why couldn't it have been his right arm, so he'd be able to get out of writing reports for a while?

He would have landed better if something hadn't bashed him on the chin and knocked him out. The floor had buckled on impact, and a fluorescent fixture dangled nearly to the floor, but he didn't think that was what had clipped him. The briefcase the businessman had been carrying was now lying up against the elevator doors. Aha. "That briefcase cut the hell out of my chin," he said, hazarding a guess. "What's that thing made of, steel?"

"Brass trim," the guy replied.

Joe snorted. "You got a cellular phone in it, at least?"

"Yeah."

Joe would have bet a month's salary on the answer to that one. Unfortunately, he'd left his own radio in the cruiser. "Then you'd better use it. This has been great fun, but I'm due back at the station in an hour."

"I suppose almost getting killed is a big yawner for you, isn't it?" the businessman asked, an edge to his voice.

Joe almost laughed. "Killed in an elevator accident? You've been seeing too many Keanu Reeves movies. New York elevators are safer than your grandmother's rocking chair."

"Tell that to my back," said the guy in jeans. "I can't drive with a busted back, and if I can't drive, I can't pay off my rig."

"If you can't drive, you'll get an insurance settlement," the businessman said.

"And sit around doing nothing?" the trucker said. "No thanks."

Joe considered commandeering the businessman's phone and calling in the accident himself but when the businessman picked up the phone to call, Joe figured he might as well continue. Anyway, with his luck the phone was some upscale model that required either a Ph.D. or the mind of a seven-year-old to work it. His son Kyle loved technology—he'd even shown Joe how to program his new VCR last weekend. Joe wouldn't have bought the thing except Kyle liked to rent movies on the rare occasions he spent time with Joe. And they were always the same movies—*Star Trek* I through VI. The kid loved Spock.

"They're sending a team to get us out," the businessman said, snapping the phone closed.

*Beam me up, Scotty,* Joe thought just as the elevator rumbled and lurched to the right.

"Damn!" the trucker yelled. "Aren't we all the way down yet?"

"We're all the way down," Joe said. "The blasted thing's still settling, that's all. Move all your fingers and toes, see if you still have your motor coordination." In the silence, Joe said a little prayer for the trucker. Paralysis was a tough hand to be dealt.

"I can move everything," the trucker said.

"Good. What's your name?"

"Lavette. Chase Lavette."

"T. R. McGuinnes," said the businessman.

"Joe Gilardini," Joe supplied. "I wish I could say it was nice to meet you guys, but under the circumstances I wish I'd been denied the pleasure."

"Same here," Lavette said.

McGuinnes remained silent. "Either one of you ever been out West?" he asked a few minutes later.

"Why do you want to know?" Lavette asked.

"I don't, really. I just think talking is better than sitting around waiting for the elevator to shift again."

"Guess you're right," Lavette said. "No, I've never been out West. Eastern Seaboard's my route. Always wanted to go out there, though."

Joe sighed. "God, so have I. The wide-open spaces. Peace and quiet."

"No elevators," Lavette added.

Joe smiled in the darkness. The trucker had a sense of humor. "Yeah. If I didn't have my kid living in New York, I'd turn in my badge, collect my pension and go." But he didn't dare leave town with Darlene's rich lawyer hubby filing petitions to legally adopt Kyle. Joe had been on his way up to his lawyer's office to discuss the reply to that petition. "Hell, no," hadn't been quite the reply his lawyer had recommended, but that was the tone Joe wanted to convey to Emerson J. Pope, alias Kyle's stepfather.

Joe had met the esteemed Mr. Pope once. He dressed a lot like McGuinnes and was the kind of stuffed shirt who could give Kyle video games by the truckload, send him to space camp and computer camp and quite possibly turn him into a nerd.

"I just heard about this guest ranch in Arizona that's up for sale," McGuinnes said, breaking into Joe's thoughts. "One of those working guest ranches with a small herd of cattle. I'm going out there next week to look it over."

Lavette leapt on it. "No kidding? Think you might buy it?"

"If it checks out."

"Running a guest ranch." Joe smoothed his mustache. "You know, that wouldn't be half-bad." God, he'd love to take Kyle out to a place like that, let him ride horses and play in the sunshine like a real boy for a change. A father and son could really get to know each other on a ranch .

"And after I've had some fun with it, I'll sell it for a nice profit," McGuinnes continued. "The city's growing in that direction, and in a couple of years developers will be crying to get their hands on that land, all one hundred and sixty acres of it. I can't lose."

"A hundred and sixty acres," Lavette said.

Joe liked the sound of it, himself, although he wondered why McGuinnes was telling them all this.

"I'm looking for partners," McGuinnes said.

Joe laughed. That answered his question, all right. "Now I've heard everything. Only in New York would a guy use an accident as a chance to set up a deal." The elevator settled with another metallic groan, jostling Joe's bad arm. He grimaced.

"Would you rather sit here and think about the elevator collapsing on us?" McGuinnes asked.

"I'd rather think about your ranch," Lavette said. "I'd go in on it in a minute if I had the cash."

"You might get that settlement," McGuinnes said.

"You know, I might."

Joe listened with interest. No question that McGuinnes was a born deal-maker, which was probably why he had lots of money and Joe didn't.

"Listen, McGuinnes," Lavette said. "After we get out of here, let's keep in touch. You never know."

"I guarantee you wouldn't go wrong with this investment. The Sun Belt's booming."

"I think you're both nutcases," Joe said, but underneath his sarcasm he wasn't so sure. All his life he'd struggled with finances, but he just didn't seem to have a talent for making money. McGuinnes obviously did. Besides that, a ranch in Arizona sounded damned appealing right now. Emerson J. Pope didn't have a ranch in Arizona, now, did he?

"So you're not interested?" McGuinnes asked.

Oh, he was smooth, Joe thought. "I didn't say that. Hell, what else is there to be interested in down in this hole? If the ranch looks good, just call the Forty-third

Precinct and leave a message for me." He calculated his unused sick and vacation days. That would raise a chunk of money. If he took out a loan using his pension as collateral, he might be able to get in on this deal. Then again, it was taking a hell of a financial risk.

McGuinnes stirred. "Let me get some business cards out of my briefcase."

"I'd just as soon not think about your briefcase, McGuinnes," Joe said. "Let's talk some more about the ranch. What's the name of it, anyway? I always liked those old ranch names—the Bar X, the Rocking J. Remember 'Bonanza'?"

"I saw that on reruns," Lavette said. "The guy I liked was Clint Eastwood. I snuck in to see *High Plains Drifter* at least six times when I was a kid. Back then, I would have given anything to be a cowboy."

"Yeah, me, too," Joe admitted. "So what's the place called?"

McGuinnes didn't answer right away. "Well, this spread is named something a little different," he said at last.

"Yeah?" Gilardini said. "What could be so different?"

"The True Love Ranch."

JOE SAT at a fork in the dirt road, his 1983 Chevy Cavalier groaning from an overworked air conditioner. Kyle sat perched in the passenger seat, a model of the bridge of the *Enterprise* on his lap. He wore new cowboy boots, jeans, a snazzy Western shirt and Spock ears. He'd worn those damned ears the entire road trip from New York. Joe was afraid some sort of fungus might be growing under them, but every time he tried to coax them off, Kyle had a fit.

At the fork in the road a wooden sign indicated Corrals to the left and Main House to the right. Underneath each sign was burned what was apparently the True Love's official brand, a heart with an arrow through it. Joe stared at the heart and stroked his mustache. And he'd hoped to make a man out of his son in this place.

"What ya say we check out the corrals first, son?" he asked, figuring that would set the right tone for the visit.

Kyle shrugged. "I guess."

"Before we do, how about if you take off your Spock ears and put on that cowboy hat I gave you?"

Kyle clapped his hands over the pointy ears.

"Come on, Kyle. Cowboys don't have Spock ears."

"I'm not a cowboy." Kyle's blue eyes grew stormy. "I'm the second in command of the starship *Enterprise*."

"Okay, let's pretend we just beamed down to the planet Arizona, where everybody wears cowboy hats and boots, and you're here on a secret mission, so you have to look like the natives."

Kyle craned around in his seat and surveyed the unfamiliar trees, bushes and prickly cactus plants. Then he gazed up at the craggy mountains towering above them. "It looks a lot different from home, that's for sure."

"That's because it's the planet Arizona." Joe reached over to the back seat and picked up the black hat he'd bought for Kyle the week before, a miniature version of the one he was wearing. "Here. Just take off the ears, and—"

"Nope." Kyle pressed his hands against his ears and shook his head.

Joe sighed.

Kyle peered up at him, looking worried. "Are you mad at me, Dad?"

"No, not really."

"I'll wear the hat *with* the ears." Joe handed him the hat and watched him position it carefully, so that the ears curved up against the underside of the brim.

He glanced at his father. "How's that?"

It wasn't exactly how Joe had pictured Kyle looking when the boy stepped foot on the ranch where his father was one-third owner, but it would have to do. "Fine," he said, and turned the wheel toward the left.

He'd never had much use for planes—total lack of control—so he'd decided to drive out to Arizona from New York. That way he could also see some of the country and give himself more time to spend with Kyle. McGuinnes hadn't liked that. He'd wanted Joe to come out immediately to investigate the "incidents" they were having on the True Love. Joe figured McGuinnes was letting the excitement of the wild West fire his imagination. Besides, Joe was officially retired from police work, but McGuinnes had claimed that Joe needed to protect his investment. He was a persistent son-of-a-gun, Joe had to admit. McGuinnes had pursued the purchase of this ranch and the financial cooperation of his partners with a single-mindedness that impressed Joe.

And he'd married the foreman, Freddy Singleton. Lavette had tied the knot recently, too—some gal from New York he'd accidentally gotten pregnant during a wild night in his truck cab. "You guys are taking this True Love name a little too literally, aren't you?" Joe had commented when he'd heard about Lavette. "You got aphrodisiacs in the well water or something?"

"Maybe. Wait'll you see Freddy's sister, Leigh."

"Hey, that's the *last* thing I'm looking for when I come out there."

"Then you'd better stick to beer," McGuinnes had said, laughing.

The corrals came into view, solid fences of weathered tree branches laid on top of each other between parallel supports. Beyond the corrals was a metal-sided barn with two wings, one made of the same sheet metal and the other, looking older, built of rock. Several pickup trucks clustered around the barn and corrals, and something was obviously happening. Cowboys were hanging on the fence, and considerable dust was rising from inside.

Joe drove partway into the clearing and parked the Chevy under the shade of a feathery-leaved tree with green bark. "Let's go see what's going on," he said. He was all the way around the car before Kyle climbed reluctantly from his seat. Joe scooped him up and held him so he could see into the large corral to their right, where about twenty horses milled around or stood and dozed. Joe felt a rush of pride. Those were his horses. He was standing on his land. He took a deep whiff of dry desert air scented with horse manure. No car exhaust. No rotting garbage. It had taken all of his unused sick leave, all his vacation pay and a big chunk of each monthly retirement check, but it was worth it. "Pretty good-looking animals in that corral, wouldn't you say?"

"They're big."

"They won't seem so big when you get used to them," Joe said. From the far corral came shouts of encouragement from the cowboys lining the fence. He put Kyle down and took his hand. "Come on. Let's go over there and find out what the fuss is all about."

As they started across the clearing, brakes screeched behind them. Joe turned quickly to make sure the vehicle was under control, and saw both doors of a dark blue pickup fly open. A blonde leapt from the driver's side and a brunette from the passenger's side.

"Ry's going to kill me for telling you about this!" shouted the blonde.

"I would have killed you if you hadn't!" the brunette shouted back.

Neither paid any attention to Joe and Kyle as they raced for the far corral.

"Daddy, who are those ladies?" Kyle asked as they followed the two women across the dirt yard.

"I think those are the Singleton sisters," Joe said. Even running pell-mell across the clearing, they lived up to McGuinnes's description. Freddy, the brunette, was the taller of the two. Leigh, the head wrangler for the True Love, had the more voluptuous figure.

Kyle pointed to Freddy as she ran toward the corral, her boots kicking up little explosions of dust. "That one is real mad."

"I think—"

"Ry McGuinnes, don't you dare!" Freddy pulled herself up on the fence and leaned forward. "Get off of there this minute!"

Joe wondered who the hell Ry was until suddenly he remembered that T.R. had officially changed his name, saying that Ry suited him better now that he lived in the West.

That wasn't all that had changed about McGuinnes, Joe decided as he neared the corral. A makeshift bucking chute had been constructed on the left side of the structure. McGuinnes—a tanner, leaner McGuinnes in worn jeans, a dirt-stained Western shirt and a battered cowboy hat—crouched above the chute, ready to lower himself to the broad back of a Brahma bull.

McGuinnes flicked a glance over at Freddy, his bride, and touched the brim of his hat in salute. Then he lowered himself to the bull's back and gave the signal to open the gate.

"You idiot!" yelled Freddy, and smacked her hat on the ground.

Leigh climbed onto the fence for a better view. Her backside wasn't far from Joe's cheek, but she didn't acknowledge his presence. All her attention was focused on the man and animal in the bucking chute.

Joe followed the direction of her gaze as the bull stood trembling for a moment, then hurled itself into the corral. Cowboys cheered as the bull spun around, the bell strapped to its chest clanging like a fire alarm. Then the animal bucked and landed forefeet first while it kicked out viciously with its hind legs. McGuinnes whooped and stayed on.

Across the corral Joe spied Lavette. The ex-trucker was yelling and punching his fist in the air. Lavette looked different, too—bigger, stronger. Ranch life had also treated him well, it seemed.

The bull spun again, its eyes wild, with mucus flying from its nostrils. All four feet came off the ground at the same time, and when they landed, Joe winced at the jarring impact.

"Ride him, McGuinnes!" Leigh shouted.

McGuinnes stayed on.

"Dad." Kyle pulled on his hand. "What's happening?"

Joe picked him up so he could see. "My partner is riding that bull," he said with a wide grin. Ranch life was going to be more fun than he'd thought.

Kyle took one look at the heaving, snorting animal and buried his face in Joe's shoulder, nudging off his hat. "I wanna go home!"

"Kyle, it's okay."

Leigh glanced briefly in his direction.

"It's like a rodeo," Joe continued, embarrassed by Kyle's reaction. He was seven, after all—old enough to handle something like this. "Haven't you seen rodeos on TV?"

The bull bellowed and lifted itself into the air with the grace of Michael Jordan making a jump shot. Still in the air, it twisted, and that twist sent McGuinnes flying. Joe tensed.

"Daddy," Kyle whimpered, still hiding against Joe's shoulder. "I wanna go! I'm scared."

McGuinnes hit the dirt hard. He didn't move.

"Get that bull away from him!" yelled Freddy, who was already climbing the fence as if she intended to play the part of rodeo clown herself.

A grizzled cowboy grabbed her by the belt and pulled her off the fence. "I'll git him," he drawled. He was inside the corral in record time and whistling to get the bull's attention. "Haul Ry outa there while I supervise this critter!" he called to the cowboys at the opposite side of the corral.

"Gotcha, Duane," someone yelled.

Duane taunted the bull, waving his hat like a matador's cape to get the bull to charge. Meanwhile, the other cowboys hauled a groggy McGuinnes to his feet and helped him over the fence.

"He's safe!" shouted a cowboy to Duane.

"I don't need to be told twice." Duane feinted left and charged right, leaping for the safety of the fence only inches ahead of the bull. He scrambled over right in front of Joe, who stepped aside and held tight to a quivering Kyle.

"'Scuse me," Duane said. "That bull's a bit upset."

As if to underscore the statement, the bull bellowed and charged the fence at the point where Duane had just climbed over. Wood splintered and flew in all directions as the fence gave way.

With another bellow, the bull charged through the opening and veered, coming straight at Joe.

# 2

SPLIT-SECOND TIMING was Joe's specialty. In one unbroken motion he hoisted a screaming Kyle up to Leigh and reached for his gun. Except there was no gun.

With a curse, he leapt aside just as the bull charged. People yelled all around him, but he ignored the noise and focused on the animal, which for some perverse reason had chosen him as a target. The bull whirled and Joe headed for the first available cover, the far side of his road-weary Chevy.

As the bull bellowed and charged, he realized his mistake. He should have hurled himself behind the ranch truck, instead.

The rampaging animal hit the passenger side with a crunch of metal and an explosion of glass. At the moment of impact, Joe remembered with deep regret that he'd dropped his comprehensive insurance coverage. The Cavalier rocked but didn't go over. He eased up and looked through the shattered window to discover the bull, apparently unhurt, backing up and pawing the ground as if preparing for another charge.

Before the bull could accomplish more vehicular damage, two ropes sailed out. One settled around its horns and the second looped one hind foot. A moment later, a third loop dropped over its horns and a fourth snagged his other hind foot. Joe recognized Duane stretching one of the ropes. Equally experienced-looking cowboys held tight to the other three. Joe cautiously stood up behind his car.

"Git the bull rope and strap off him," Duane said, directing a fifth cowboy who moved in on the wild-eyed bull. "That'll settle him down some."

Joe noticed with some surprise that the fifth cowboy was Lavette. The ex-trucker deftly removed the chest rope holding the bell and another strap down by the bull's genitals. When Joe saw where the second strap had been chafing the bull, he figured the animal had a right to be mad as hell. Joe just wished he'd picked a different target.

As Duane led a considerably more docile bull away, Lavette glanced toward Joe, then gazed at the car. The passenger door was caved in and the window glass sprayed over the interior. Lavette shook his head. "Welcome to the True Love," he said in a rough imitation of Lorne Greene.

Joe cleared his throat. "You folks know how to do it up right. Is McGuinnes okay?"

"He's fine now, but I wouldn't give you two cents for his hide after Freddy's through with him."

"I'd better go see about my kid." Joe glanced toward the corral where Leigh Singleton was climbing down, Kyle still in her arms.

Leigh. He recalled that in that sliver of a second when he'd handed Kyle up, her gaze had locked with his. It had probably been just the drama of the moment that had given their exchanged glance such importance. But in that moment when he'd entrusted Kyle to her, he'd imagined...no, that was stupid. He didn't believe in any of that New Age nonsense about fate. He started across the clearing.

Kyle had a hammerlock on Leigh's neck as he looked fearfully from the departing bull to the smashed car. Once the bull was out of sight behind the barn, Leigh said something to Kyle and gave him a squeeze. Then she lowered him to the ground and retrieved his hat. When she tried to hand it to him, he shook his head and started toward Joe at a run.

Joe cursed to himself. This little episode wasn't going to help Kyle adjust to ranch life. The child could easily demand to go home this very minute. As Kyle came nearer, Joe squatted so he'd be at his son's eye level. He greeted Kyle with a nonchalant smile. "Pretty exciting stuff, huh?"

Kyle regarded him with a solemn expression. His voice came out as a whisper. "He smashed our car, Dad."

"Nah. Just a little dent." Over Kyle's shoulder Joe could see Leigh approaching with Kyle's hat in her hand. "I can pound it out."

"Dad, can I go—"

"Listen, Kyle." Joe hoped to avoid the embarrassment of having everyone witness his son begging to leave the ranch. He clasped Kyle by the shoulders and gazed into his eyes. "I know this was a little scary, but don't bail out on me yet, okay? I think if you give this place a try, you'll like it a lot."

Kyle fidgeted. "But, I—"

"We drove all the way out here to see Arizona." Joe's impatience grew as he longed to instill some grit in the timid boy. "You don't want to turn around and go back before you know what ranch life is like, do you?"

Kyle's soft blue gaze looked distressed. "But can I go—"

"Just a week, Kyle. Give it a week. Seven days. I know you can do that."

"But can I go to the *bathroom*?"

Leigh's soft chuckle let Joe know she'd heard most of the exchange. Feeling like a fool, he glanced up, straight into her liquid brown eyes. And he forgot to breathe.

"I have to go really *bad*," Kyle said, hopping up and down.

"Okay, buddy." Joe stood, commanding himself to look away from Leigh's compelling gaze. Damn. And he hadn't even had a sip of the well water around here yet.

"You can take him into the bunkhouse," Leigh said.

"Where's that?"

"Right over there." She pointed toward a one-story rock building that reminded Joe of an army barracks. "Want me to take him?"

"No." Joe glanced at her but didn't allow himself to fall headfirst into that deep gaze again. "I mean, no, thanks. And I really appreciate your grabbing him when the bull broke through the fence. Not everyone has that kind of quick reaction in an emergency."

"No problem." She held out her hand. "I'm Leigh Singleton. You must be Joe."

"That's right." He'd been shaking hands with women ever since he'd hit puberty. Sometimes he'd felt the sensuous pull of a potential lover in the simple gesture, sometimes just the touch of a future friend. But when he enclosed Leigh's hand in his, a connection was made that surged through him with the power of a .357 Magnum. Drawn back into the fathomless mystery of her eyes, he was stunned into speechlessness.

"I...I'm sorry about your car." Her voice had a husky edge to it, as if she felt the incredible energy between them, too. Whether she did or not, she hadn't pulled her hand away and he seemed incapable of releasing it.

"It just needs a little bodywork," Joe said. Bodywork. Two bodies, working together in perfect—

"Daddy!" Kyle grabbed his arm and forced Joe's attention back to his son.

If he hadn't, Joe wondered if he would have remembered Kyle was even there. "Sure thing." He released

Leigh's hand and looked down at the boy, who was holding his crotch and dancing around.

"Here's his hat," Leigh said, handing it to Joe.

"Thanks. Guess I'll be seeing you around."

"Considering the condition of your car, you'll need a lift to the house. I can take you if you want."

"Sure." He twirled Kyle's hat, trying for nonchalance, and had to make a grab for it as it flipped out of his hand. "That would be great."

"I'll be here."

"Great." With Kyle tugging on his arm, he sort of backed away from her and damn near tripped himself up before he finally turned around and walked to the bunkhouse facing forward, like a sane person. That's what he'd been until five minutes ago. He'd embarrassed himself badly. After all, he was a man who would turn forty-two in November, a man who'd taken several women to bed and been married for six years. He considered himself experienced when it came to women. He considered himself in control. He'd never believed in attraction more powerful than reason.

Until now.


LEIGH TOOK a deep breath and fingered the crystal hanging on a velvet cord around her neck. Her whole body was on red alert. She'd always known this would happen to her someday, but she'd never have guessed the feeling would be brought on by a New York cop. Funny thing was, with his jeans, boots and a Stetson, he looked more like Pat Garrett or Wyatt Earp, especially with the fresh scar across his chin. Leigh could easily imagine him facing down a gunslinger. She pictured how his steel gray eyes would narrow as his face became an impenetrable mask. Not even a twitch of his mustache would betray him until the moment a gun appeared in his hand.

Leigh shivered. If this was the man with whom she was psychically linked, the cosmos certainly had a sense of humor.

"Hey, Leigh!"

She turned to face Ry, who was walking unsteadily toward her. Remembering that he might be angry because she'd told Freddy about his decision to ride the bull, she held up both hands. "Look, she was suspicious and finally asked me a direct question about whether you planned to ride that bull today. You know I'm no good at lying, especially to my own sister."

"Oh, that." He dismissed the topic with a wave of his hand. "It'll blow over."

"I don't see her hanging on your arm like an adoring bride."

"No, I think she caught a ride back to the house with Lavette. Said something about not wanting to ride in any vehicle I was driving."

Leigh repressed a smile. "Then I guess it hasn't blown over yet."

"It will. She has something more important on her mind than me riding a bull, as I'm sure you know."

"I do?"

Ry stared at her in astonishment. "She didn't tell you?"

"How should I know? I don't even know what you're talking about. I think getting thrown from that bull addled your brains."

Ry took off his hat and ran his fingers through his sweat-matted hair. "I figured she'd tell you first." A smile softened his lips. "But apparently, she didn't. I'll be damned."

"Will you tell me what the heck you're babbling about?"

Ry adjusted his hat and looked at her with a jubilant light in his eyes. "Freddy's pregnant."

Leigh whooped and launched herself at him, forgetting he'd been thrown from a bull not long ago. "I knew it!"

Ry groaned and set her gently away from him. "You did?"

"Well, I didn't *know*, in the sense that she'd told me, but I had a feeling. She made a mysterious trip into town yesterday, but she didn't tell me why."

"Oh." Ry's pleased expression returned. "Then I must have been the first one she told."

"She told you just now, after the bull ride?"

He looked sheepish. "I think she was planning to save the news for a more romantic moment, like over dinner in La Osa or a moonlight ride out to the pond. Instead, it sort of—came out. I was a little groggy, but I vaguely remember her saying that a man who was about to become a father had no business risking his ass on a bull. Something like that."

Leigh chuckled. "At least you still were the first to know."

"Yeah," he said softly. "I like that. By the way, where did Joe and his son go? I saw you talking to them, but by the time I looked over here again, he was gone."

"He took Kyle to the bathroom in the bunkhouse. I'm sure they'll be back any minute."

"Good. When they get back, will you distract his son for a little bit? I want to show Joe the corral fence, and there's no point in scaring that little kid any more than we have already."

A familiar dread gripped Leigh. "What's scary about the fence?" She could almost predict what he was about to say. The corrals were nearly a century old, but they were strong. A solid wall of mesquite shouldn't splinter and give way, not even when assaulted by an angry bull.

"Some of the branches were sawed through," Ry said. "Not just at that point, but in several places. I need to get Lavette down here with me later on today to check all the corrals."

Leigh's stomach clenched at the thought that someone had taken a saw to the mesquite logs, which had been framing the True Love corrals for generations. "Why don't you ask Duane to do it?"

Ry blew out a breath. "Because I can't trust him."

"Ry! Duane just saved your ungrateful hide from that bull!"

"I know." Ry looked unhappy. "He's the one who taught me how to ride him, too."

"Not to mention the fact that he's our top hand. I've known him for fifteen years, and he's not capable of something like that."

"Depends on how threatened he feels by the idea of us selling the ranch to developers one day. If he hates the idea as much as I think he does, he has a motive, and he sure as heck has the opportunity. I think that Joe will agree that—" He paused and glanced over Leigh's shoulder. "Well, here comes our investigator, now. How're you doing, Joe?"

Joe grasped his hand. "You know, McGuinnes, every time I'm around you, things coming flying at me. First your briefcase and now your Brahma bull. It's an upsetting pattern."

Goose bumps rose on Leigh's arms at the sound of his voice. It's timbre resonated through her, as if she'd been listening to it all her life. Her first impulse was to stare at him. To avoid doing that, she focused on Kyle, who had his hat back on with the Spock ears poking out under the brim.

"Romeo's your bull, too," Ry said to Joe with a grin. "Just let me know when you're ready to ride him."

"I should have guessed the True Love would have a bull named Romeo."

Leigh thrust her hands into her hip pockets. "He was already named when my dad won him in a poker game," she said.

Joe glanced at her. "I suppose you'd call that fate."

"I suppose I would." She could feel him testing the link between them the way a high-wire artist tests a tight-rope.

"We've considered selling him," Ry said, "but the guests like to have their pictures taken with him."

"And every once in a while some fool climbs aboard to prove his manhood," Leigh added.

Joe nodded and looked at Ry. "I'll admit I was impressed. From the bull market to a real live bull is quite a stretch for a commodities broker, wouldn't you say?"

"Wait until you've been here a while," Ry said. "This place inspires you."

"I'm sure Joe's not crazy enough to follow your example." Leigh said that for Kyle's sake, but in actuality she figured Joe was at least that crazy. She sensed he was attracted to risk, and for all his feigned nonchalance she'd bet he was already picturing himself on that bull. He probably didn't even realize his son was standing next to him trembling with fear at the same picture. To end the discussion, she implemented Ry's plan. "Listen, I know you two have a few things to catch up on, so why don't Kyle and I unload your car and put everything into the back of my truck while you talk?"

"Great idea," Ry said. "As a matter of fact, I did want to consult with you, Joe. Something's happened concerning that subject I mentioned when I asked you to come out here."

Joe hesitated and glanced at Kyle. "Is that okay with you, son?"

"Daddy, you aren't gonna ride that...that Romeo, are you?"

"Not today, that's for sure."

"You might ride him some other day?"

Joe put a hand on his son's shoulder. "I doubt that, Kyle. Don't worry about it. I'd appreciate your helping Miss Singleton get our stuff while I talk to Mr. Mc-Guinnes."

"You mean her?" Kyle pointed to Leigh.

"Yes. Miss Singleton."

"She said to call her Leigh."

"Oh." Joe's glance flicked to Leigh and she nodded. "Okay." He dug in his pocket for the car keys and handed them to her. "Thanks, Leigh."

She'd waited a lifetime to hear her name spoken with that subtle intonation that hinted of future passion. "You're welcome." She took the keys, her fingers brushing his. The texture of his skin was tantalizingly familiar. As she'd have expected, the key ring was plain with no whimsical identification hanging from it. A unicorn dangled on her key chain. "Come on, Kyle." Leigh held out her hand, and after another apprehensive look in his father's direction, Kyle put his hand in hers. As she started away from Joe, she could feel his gaze on her and knew from an abrupt absence of warmth the very moment he turned away and returned his attention to Ry.

"I take it you like 'Star Trek,'" she said to Kyle as they neared the battered car.

He nodded vigorously.

"How about 'The Next Generation'?"

Kyle glanced up at her in surprise. "Have you seen that show?"

"Yes. I didn't watch all the episodes, but I've seen a few."

"I've seen them *all* but what I like best is the movies."

"And your favorite character is Spock."

Kyle's eyes widened. "How did you know?" When she smiled, understanding dawned on his face. "Oh, yeah. My ears."

"That was my first clue."

"Dad wanted me to take them off, but I didn't."

"You mean those aren't your real ears?"

He giggled. "No. 'Course not. I'm not a Vulcan really."

"Well, they *look* real."

"They sure do." He gazed up at her with the sunniest expression she'd seen since he arrived. "You know what I have in the car?" he said. "The bridge of the *Enterprise!* I'll show it to you." He started to pull away from her.

"Wait a minute, Kyle." She gently tugged him back. "Let me go inside the car first. There's broken glass, and I don't want either of us to get cut." She led him around to the driver's side of the Cavalier and opened the door.

"It should be on the seat." Kyle bounced around behind her, trying to see inside. "That's where I left it."

"Let me check." Leigh picked a couple of pieces of glass from the driver's seat and put her knee down gingerly. When no hidden glass bit into it, she held the passenger seat headrest for balance and leaned over, searching for Kyle's toy. Nothing occupied the seat but a shower of glass.

"Do you see it?"

"Not yet. I'm looking." She peered on the floor, but only found more glass, a discarded Big Mac box and a map. With a sinking sensation in her stomach, she leaned farther across the seat so that she could see into the caved-in space between the seat and the door. A crumpled piece of multicolored plastic was wedged there. She'd never seen a model of the bridge of the *Enterprise,* but she was pretty sure she was looking at the ruins of one now.

"Is it in there?" His voice was pitched higher now, as if he'd guessed the fate of his treasure.

She longed to tell him she couldn't find it, unload the trunk and let Joe handle this. She backed out of the car and crouched to Kyle's level. "I'm afraid the bridge is done for, Kyle. It fell between the seat and door, and when the bull—"

"I wanna see!" He made a lunge for the interior of the car and she caught him just in time. "I wanna see!" he cried again, struggling in her arms.

"You can't. There's glass everywhere. I'm sorry, Kyle."

"Spock is in there!" From Kyle's tragic wail Leigh could almost imagine Leonard Nimoy himself squashed in the wreckage.

"We'll get him out," she said, holding fast to the squirming boy. "But it might take a crowbar to get that door open. And I don't know what you'll find."

Sobbing, Kyle collapsed against her. "My bridge. My bridge."

Leigh held him as tears misted her own eyes. Poor little guy. He'd have a hard time living up to the rough-and-tough image his father seemed to hold in such esteem.

"What's he crying about now?"

She glanced up to see Joe standing less than a yard away, his legs braced apart, his hands bracketing his hips, his expression clearly annoyed. But it was his use of "now" that set her off. "He just discovered his favorite toy was smashed in the door when the bull charged," she snapped. "And he has every right to cry about that, in my opinion."

Joe's eyes narrowed, just as she'd imagined they would when facing down a gunslinger. "I don't remember asking your opinion. Kyle, come here."

Kyle slowly disengaged himself from Leigh's arms, turned and walked toward his father, his head bowed.

Joe crouched. "We'll get another bridge, Kyle."

Kyle sniffed. "I want Spock," he said brokenly.

"Stop crying and be a big boy."

Leigh clenched her teeth in frustration. She glanced around for Ry, but he must have found an errand elsewhere. She'd have to deal with Mr. Macho on her own.

"I want Spock!" Kyle cried.

"We'll get another Spock."

Kyle's head came up as if his father had uttered a blasphemy. "No, Daddy! We have to get him out!"

"Kyle, it's just a plastic—"

"Oh, for heaven's sake." Leigh stormed around the car and grabbed the handle. Focusing all her strength on the task, she yanked the door. It came open, the remaining window glass tinkling as it spilled to the dirt. A little figure in a blue tunic toppled out. She picked him up. He had a couple of nicks, but at least he wasn't missing any body parts.

Joe had come around the car, Kyle's hand firmly gripped in his. Leigh avoided his gaze as she handed the tiny figure to Kyle.

"Thanks, Leigh," he whispered, holding Spock against his chest. Then his glance fell on the mangled bridge smashed up against the seat and his lower lip trembled.

"That's enough, Kyle. Go on over by the blue truck while we unload the car."

The little boy started over. Once, he turned back and gazed with grief-stricken eyes at his beloved bridge, but at a nod from Joe he trudged on.

"Don't you see that it's more than just a piece of plastic to him?" Leigh asked.

"That's what bothers me. He's in tears at the drop of a hat."

"And I don't suppose you've ever cried, have you?"

"Not since I was a lot younger than he is. Not that it's any of your business, if you'll pardon my being blunt."

"If you'll pardon my being blunt, Kyle is nothing like you. He's a sensitive, imaginative little soul who needs careful nurturing."

His jaw muscles tensed. "If he is, it's because he's been mollycoddled."

"I suppose you consider what I just did mollycoddling?"

"Yes." When she started to protest, he cut her off.

"Kyle is my son," he said with fierce emphasis. "*My son.*"

"You sound as if I mean to take him away from you!"

"That's ridiculous!" He walked quickly past her toward the car. "We're wasting time. Let's get the stuff out of the trunk."

Her anger drained away. So *that* was it. Although he'd moved rapidly to hide his response, she'd seen the flash of stark fear in his eyes. He was a divorced father afraid of losing touch with his only child. Leigh wondered if it had already happened, or if fate had tossed them all together just in the nick of time.

# 3

As Joe rode with Leigh and Kyle up to the ranch house, rainbows flashed in his face from the crystal she'd hung from the rearview mirror. Damned distracting and probably a road hazard, he thought. He'd noticed a rainbow painted on the fender, and a unicorn hung from her key chain, swaying with every jolt of the rutted dirt road. So she was into the New Age scene. Next she'd be asking him what sign he was born under so she could figure out why he was such a mean father.

He wondered if things could possibly be worse. Kyle was afraid of everything about the ranch, except, of course, for his new idol, Leigh Singleton. As they drove, Leigh pointed out a jackrabbit and a roadrunner to Kyle, who seemed entranced with every observation Leigh made. Joe would be lucky if he'd get any time alone with the kid now. Kyle would be Leigh's shadow for the next week.

On top of that, Joe had begun to believe there really was a sabotage problem at the True Love. Apparently, he'd given up New York felons in exchange for Arizona saboteurs. Had he really been naive enough to imagine he'd find a different world out here? And his car was smashed in, not to mention Kyle's favorite toy. He'd felt bad about that, but pampering Kyle wouldn't help the kid grow up. The world was a rough place, but Kyle wouldn't learn that from Emerson J. Pope. Teaching Kyle those lessons was up to Joe.

"Did Ry send you any pictures of the ranch house?" Leigh asked, glancing at Joe.

"No." He decided to tack on a little more explanation so he wouldn't sound belligerent. Leigh had already caused him to display his feelings more than he cared to. "But he did describe it as whitewashed adobe, so I have a mental picture."

"Leigh, what's adobe?" Kyle asked.

Joe noticed which adult Kyle asked for information.

"It's building blocks made of mud and straw," she said. "In the old days, they baked the blocks in the sun, but now they fire them the way you would a clay pot."

"Could I make some adobe blocks and bake them in the sun?"

"Sure. I mean—" She shot a look at Joe. "We'll have to see how the time works out. I'm sure you have a lot of things planned to do with your father."

"Not really."

Joe clenched his jaw. "Leigh's a busy lady, Kyle. She's the head wrangler for the ranch, which means she has to take care of all the horses. I don't know if she'll have time to—"

"I have time." Her voice had an edge to it.

Joe felt as if she'd just drawn a line in the sand with the toe of her boot. "So do I," he said.

"So do I!" chortled Kyle. "We can all do it together."

A dry chuckle came from Leigh's side of the cab. Then she steered the truck around a bend in the road and the ranch house came into view. "Well, here we are."

A small smile of satisfaction came unbidden to Joe's lips. The graceful one-story ranch house, shaded across the front with a wide porch, looked exactly as he'd pictured it. Pots of red geraniums and a line of cane chairs occupied the porch, although no one was sitting there in the heat of early afternoon.

"That's a big house," Kyle said. "How many people live in it?"

"That depends." Leigh parked the truck in front of a low wall that embraced a front yard of grass and two large trees. "We don't have many guests this time of year. August is always slow. But when all the guest rooms are full, we have close to sixty people here."

"Then it's just like an apartment," Kyle said. "Only stretched out flat instead of stacked up."

Leigh turned to him and smiled. "That's right. We have room to stretch out on the True Love."

She had a way with double meanings, Joe thought. And that smile. He'd never seen one quite like it. It warmed and welcomed, yet hinted of untold secrets. He was a sucker for secrets.

"Belinda makes the best lemonade in the valley," Leigh said, opening the door of the truck. "Who's ready for some?"

"Me!" Kyle said. "Who's Belinda?"

"She's been in charge of the kitchen for more than fifty years."

"Wow." Kyle slipped under the steering wheel and got out on Leigh's side. "I need my backpack."

"I'll get it," Joe volunteered. "You two go ahead. I'll bring the suitcases." He wanted some time alone to savor the setting as well as a few minutes to neutralize Leigh's effect on him. In spite of his earlier anger and her instant camaraderie with Kyle, he was drawn to her. If he didn't exercise some care, he'd soon be following her around just like his son.

He watched the two of them go up the flagstone walk as if they'd known each other for years. Kyle grabbed

Leigh's hand and pointed, with obvious excitement, to a pair of cottontails munching on the grass. Crouching next to him, Leigh said something Joe couldn't hear and Kyle nodded solemnly. His heart heavy, Joe turned away and walked around to the truck's tailgate to retrieve the luggage. Kyle was supposed to be responding to him like that, instead of to some woman who had been a stranger only two hours earlier.

He slung Kyle's backpack—a Star Trek model, of course—over one shoulder and hefted a suitcase in each hand. He hadn't brought much, figuring Western clothes would be cheaper out here than back in New York. He'd sublet his apartment, leaving it furnished; it had been no trick to turn his back on that depressing little place. Leaving the station had been tougher than he'd imagined, though. He couldn't quite believe he was no longer a cop. After twenty years, it felt weird to be a civilian, to know he wouldn't be putting his life on the line every day.

But the charging bull had thrown him right back into the old adrenaline rush, and he had to admit he'd missed it. He wouldn't go back to police work just to get some excitement in his life, but becoming a bull rider... With a faint smile of anticipation, he headed up the flagstone walk.

His boots clomped satisfyingly on the wooden porch as he crossed to the heavy set of carved doors. He set down one of the suitcases, opened one of the doors and propped his shoulder against it. But as he reached down to retrieve the suitcase, Lavette appeared and grabbed it instead.

"Just in time, Joe," Lavette said. "We're trying to get everybody together so Amanda can report on the ad campaign for the True Love Rodeo."

"The what?" After some quick thinking, Joe remembered that Amanda was Lavette's wife's name, but this was the first he'd heard about a rodeo.

"We have to do something to improve business," Lavette said. "We decided to hold a rodeo." He set Joe's suitcase down on the brick-colored tile and glanced around. "What do you think of the place?"

Joe put down the other suitcase and took in the high-beamed ceiling, beehive fireplace, massive leather furniture and huge picture window looking out on a sparkling pool. To his left, through an archway, was a dining room with several rugged-looking tables flanked by ladder-back chairs. "I can't imagine why business isn't booming," he said. "This is fantastic."

Lavette lowered his voice. "It's the damned accidents. The True Love's getting a bad reputation. Ry called up here from the corrals and told me about the fence. We're hoping you—" A baby's lusty wail interrupted him. Lavette grinned and looked toward a doorway off to the right. "The kid's got a good set of lungs."

Joe recognized fatherly pride in Lavette's tone. "Must be the famous baby I've been hearing about."

"Yeah." Lavette turned to Joe and his grin widened. "That's Bart, the wonder baby, conceived in the cab of the prettiest Peterbilt you've ever seen. Amanda's in Freddy's office changing his diaper. She'll bring him out when he's decent."

Joe envied Lavette, just starting out with his son. Chase had a chance to do it right, while Joe wondered if he'd ever make up for the years he'd lost with Kyle. "Speaking of kids, where's mine?"

"Leigh shuttled him to the kitchen for lemonade and cookies."

Joe swung the backpack from his shoulders. "I'd better take him this."

"Just go through the dining room. The kitchen is beyond the swinging door on the right. The working end of the ranch house is all in that wing and the guest rooms are on the other side. While you're gone, I'll find out where these suitcases go and have them transferred."

"Thanks." Joe started toward the archway leading into the dining room.

"Joe?"

"Yeah?" Joe turned back toward Lavette.

"Maybe Belinda should keep your son in the kitchen while the rest of us talk out here. Ry's on his way up and wants to go over the incident with the fence. No use scaring your son with stories about what's been happening around the ranch."

"Sure." Joe started through the dining room and fought his irritation with Lavette. Didn't anyone credit him with any sense about being a father? Of course he wouldn't let Kyle hear their discussion. Introducing him to horses and cowboys was one thing. Exposing him to adult violence was quite another. But Lavette was new to this parenthood business and probably thought he knew more than anyone else. Joe remembered a time when he'd felt that way, too.

He pushed through the swinging door into the kitchen, a large room equipped with a commercial-size stovetop, two wall-mounted ovens, numerous cupboards and wide counters. At a small table to his right sat Leigh, Kyle and an older couple. An aluminum walker stood next to the old fellow's chair. An animated discussion came to a halt as everyone glanced up when he came in.

"Hi, Dad," Kyle said, his mouth full. "The cookies are *great*. You should have one."

"Maybe in a little while. I thought you'd want your backpack." Joe couldn't remember a time in the past three years when Kyle hadn't been frantic to have his backpack next to him.

"Sure." He put down his cookie and slid unhurriedly from his seat before coming toward Joe to take the pack. "Thanks."

Leigh stood. "Joe, I'd like you to meet Belinda and Dexter Grimes. Dexter was the foreman here for years."

"But a blood clot zapped into his brain, Dad." Kyle shouldered his backpack and walked over to stand next to the aging cowboy, who gazed at Kyle with a bemused expression. "He can understand everything, but he can't talk so good, right, Dexter?"

Dexter nodded and patted Kyle's shoulder with a gnarled hand. "Right."

Kyle looked at Leigh and Belinda. "You know, if Dexter was on the *Enterprise*, they could fix him right up."

"Kyle," Joe began, "the *Enterprise* isn't—" He'd been about to say "isn't real," until he caught Leigh's frown. "—isn't available," he finished instead, gaining Leigh's approving smile. Not that he sought that. God knows he didn't care whether she approved of him or not. But there was no need to get into an argument with Kyle in front of this nice old couple.

"It's nice to meet you, Joe." Belinda, plump and grandmotherly, had a musical voice and an angelic quality that would typecast her as a fairy godmother if such imaginary beings existed, Joe thought. And Dexter seemed like a nice old guy. Kyle obviously liked them, and Joe could see why. Kyle had struck out in the grand-parent game. Joe's folks were dead, and Darlene's parents lived in a social whirl that left them little time for their only grandchild.

"It's nice to meet both of you," Joe said. "I appreciate your making Kyle feel so at home."

"Funny things," Dexter said, touching Kyle's Spock ears.

Joe braced himself for Kyle's indignant response.

Instead, Kyle giggled. "Dexter's never *heard* of Spock." He glanced back at his father. "I'm gonna have to teach him *everything*."

"While he teaches you how to make adobe," Leigh added.

"Right," Kyle said, returning to his chair and zipping open his backpack. "Wait'll I show you what's in here, Dexter. All kinds of good stuff."

Leigh directed her gaze at Joe. "I take it we're wanted in the main room? Chase said we'd have a little meeting when you got here."

"Just leave Kyle with us," Belinda offered before Joe had a chance to ask. "I'm curious to see what's in that backpack, myself."

"You're sure he won't be any trouble?" Joe asked.

"Don't be silly." She waved him toward the door. "You and Leigh go talk about important matters with the others. We'll be fine in here."

"Thank you. Kyle, I'll be back soon, okay?"

"Okay." Kyle was digging in his pack and didn't seem the least concerned about Joe's whereabouts.

Joe held the door for Leigh and followed her out. She passed close enough that he caught a whiff of wildflowers that made his pulse race. Was there *anything* about this woman that wasn't desirable?

"They'll take good care of him," she said when the door closed.

"I have no doubt of that. It's just—" He caught himself before he said anything stupid.

She paused and looked up at him. "He's very proud of you, Joe. He told us about all of your citations for bravery from the New York Police Department."

Joe blushed, which embarrassed him more than the mention of the citations. "He found them in a drawer when I was cleaning out the apartment before we left." He damn sure didn't want her to think he'd bragged to his son about his accomplishments.

Leigh nodded. The corner of her mouth tilted up as she considered him for a moment longer. "Funny how such a brave guy can be so scared," she said softly.

"Now wait a minute. I—"

She touched his arm, effectively silencing him. "We can hash that out later. Right now we need to get this powwow over with."

Joe wondered exactly what they'd hash out, especially considering the urges flowing through him every time he looked at her. As he followed her into the main room, he marveled at how his arm still tingled where she'd laid her fingers for only a second. If he believed in magic spells, he'd swear she'd put one on him. Darlene had often complained that she'd never known what he was thinking. He had the uneasy feeling that Leigh understood his every thought.

When he and Leigh walked into the room, the other four were already seated, waiting for them. Ry and Freddy McGuinnes sat at opposite ends of a large leather sofa set at right angles to the fireplace. They weren't looking at each other, and Joe guessed the bull-riding episode was still a problem between them. Lavette sat on the arm of an overstuffed leather chair, his arm possessively draped across the back. Ensconced in the chair was a delicate-looking woman with long curly hair the color of firelight. The baby asleep on her lap had a shock of black hair like Lavette's.

Lavette stopped talking to Ry as Joe and Leigh came in. "There they are. Probably been stuffing themselves on Belinda's cookies."

From her seat on the far end of the sofa, Freddy held out her hand. "Hi, Joe. I'm Freddy. Sorry about the disaster when you arrived. It should never have happened." She flicked a glance toward Ry, who seemed not to notice.

Joe walked over to shake her hand. "I'm getting used to that kind of thing when I'm around your husband."

Ry glanced at Joe and lifted an eyebrow but said nothing.

"I'm sure glad I wasn't there," said the redhead.

"That makes two of us," Lavette said. "Joe, this is Amanda . . . and Bart." The loving tone he lavished on those two names told Joe everything he needed to know about that relationship.

Amanda smiled. "I'd shake your hand, Joe, but my arms are full."

"No problem." Joe looked around for a place to sit. All that remained in the fireplace grouping was a love seat across from the sofa. If he and Leigh shared it, they'd be quite close together. Across the room stood a table and four chairs that were probably used for card games. Joe crossed to the table, snagged one of the wooden chairs and carried it over in front of the fireplace. Turning the chair around, he straddled it and crossed his arms over the back. A quick glance told him Leigh had taken the love seat. A second glance confirmed the amusement sparkling in her brown eyes. Let her be amused, he thought. Let her consider him a coward. It was better than trying to concentrate on this meeting with her sitting inches away from him.

Ry leaned forward, hands clasped and elbows on his knees. "What do you know? All six of us in the same room at last. This is what we've needed to get the True Love on solid footing—all of us working on the problem. Amanda, what's happening with the rodeo publicity?"

Joe tried to listen to Amanda's detailing of media coverage for the rodeo, which would take place in ten days, but his attention kept straying to Leigh. She was toying with a crystal she wore around her neck on a black silk cord. When she let it go, it nestled into the unbuttoned vee of her Western shirt, a cool talisman against creamy skin that would be so warm to the touch...so warm....

"What plan of action do you propose, Joe?" Ry asked.

Joe snapped to attention. He had to assume they'd abandoned the rodeo topic and had started on the sabotage. Ignoring the laughter in Ry's expression, Joe gathered his thoughts. "You realize I've spent most of my time in uniform, not playing detective," he said.

"You're still our best hope," Lavette said. "If we call in the Pima County Sheriff's Department, we'll stir up a bucketload of publicity. You've had more experience than the rest of us, so you're elected."

A sense of excitement in the pit of his stomach told Joe he'd take on the challenge. There was a secret to be discovered. He'd complained to Ry about not wanting a working vacation, but after a long, uneventful ride in the car with Kyle, he could use some activity. The bull had taught him that. His pulse quickened as he started mapping out a strategy for catching the saboteur. "I'm not very good on a horse," he said, "and whoever investigates should probably be able to ride, so he can cover the entire ranch easily. Can somebody help me brush up on my riding skills?"

"Amanda and I can't," Lavette said. "Our plane for New York leaves in the morning, and we'll be gone a week."

Joe stared at them. "You're leaving?"

Lavette glanced down at Amanda. "The timing's not great, but we can't put it off any longer." He looked back at Joe. "We got married in a quick Las Vegas ceremony last month, and Amanda's parents are going nuts because they've never met me. That's one piece of business. The other is settling Amanda's job situation. She's going to try and convince her ad agency in New York to open a branch in Tucson and let her run it."

"Freddy and I will have our hands full getting the arena built for the rodeo," Ry said. "But Leigh's one of the best riders in the valley. She can teach you everything you need to know. She can also serve as your guide around the ranch."

The suggestion was inevitable, he thought. No matter which direction he turned, there was Leigh, singing her siren song. She was right about his being scared. He had no experience with the kind of emotions she fostered in him. She was too poised, too beautiful, too sexy. The more time he spent in her company, the better his chances of making a complete fool of himself.

"Don't forget that Joe brought his son out here for a vacation," Leigh said. "It's not fair to expect him to abandon that little boy so he can conduct our investigation."

Kyle. Joe turned to look at Leigh. In the excitement of an impending investigation, he had forgotten about his responsibility to Kyle, but Leigh hadn't. He couldn't decide if she was taunting him with his insensitivity or shining a light to direct him. Either way, she was demonstrating her superiority over him. He gritted his teeth.

"That's easily solved," Freddy said. "Leigh can teach both you and Kyle at the same time. He can go with you while you familiarize yourself with the ranch. We have a gelding named Mikey who is the gentlest, steadiest horse in the world. We'll keep him reserved for Kyle."

Joe relaxed a little. Kyle's presence would keep him from doing anything too dumb. "Sure, that'll work. I wanted Kyle to see some of the country from horseback, anyway. I hear there's bass in the pond. Maybe we can take a break for some fishing."

"That's not a bad idea," Ry said. "I'd like this investigation to be as subtle as possible. We've spread the word that you're sick of police work so that the culprits, if they're around, won't be so suspicious of you."

"Oh, they're around," Joe said. "A mysterious cattle stampede, poisoned horse-trough water, a brushfire, booby-trapped corrals—everything you've told me points to an inside job."

Freddy laughed. "Present company excluded, of course."

Joe's gaze made its way around the circle of faces. "At the beginning of an investigation, a smart cop doesn't eliminate any suspects," he said. He recorded the flash of angry fire in Leigh's eyes, and he met it with steady assessment. The investigation had begun now, as far as he was concerned, and it might as well begin with Leigh. She had as much motive as anyone. As a good cop, he had to put emotion aside and admit he really had no idea what she was capable of. Yet.

# 4

RY TRIED to make a joke out of Joe's statement . . . and failed. But after twenty years on the force, Joe was used to the kind of tension he'd just created. Unperturbed, he rose from the chair. "If somebody will tell me where Kyle and I are sleeping, I'd like to settle in there. Then I'm going back to the corrals and clean the glass out of my car."

"You're in the John Wayne Room," Freddy said sarcastically. "It's the corner room on the front of the house. We took the double bed out and put in two twins." She sounded almost resentful of the effort she'd expended on his behalf.

Joe smiled to himself. The John Wayne Room. He might not be popular now, but if he uncovered the saboteur, he'd be a hero. Unless, of course, the perp turned out to be one of the Singleton sisters. That would be messy, but he couldn't be responsible for the fallout. He'd been asked to do a job, and he intended to do it to the best of his ability.

"I'll show you where it is," Ry volunteered as the gathering dispersed.

"Okay." Joe figured Ry wanted a chance to defend his wife and sister-in-law, and he wasn't disappointed.

No sooner had they stepped into the John Wayne bedroom than Ry launched into his protest. "Listen, Freddy and Leigh have nothing to do with the sabotage. I'll vouch for them."

Joe leaned against the antique pine dresser set against one wall. "How can you?"

"Because I know them, dammit." Ry shoved his hat to the back of his head. "They would no more do these things than—"

"That's the kind of blind loyalty that muddies up clear thinking, McGuinnes. Didn't you tell me some ancestor of theirs homesteaded this place?"

"Yes, and I know what you're thinking. They'd do anything to keep it from becoming a housing development. The truth is, they *are* doing a lot to keep that from happening. They're hoping to make each of us love the place so much we aren't willing to sell."

Joe's eyes narrowed as Leigh's sexual allure took on a deeper meaning. "Is it working?"

"Well—" Ry scratched the back of his neck and glanced out the window. Then he turned back to Joe. "It's a hell of a place. It gets into your blood, changes you. You'll see what I mean in a few days."

"You mean, when Leigh's had a chance at me?"

Ry had the decency to look uncomfortable. "I'll admit Freddy and I considered that you two might hit it off, but Leigh just laughs at us. She says a New York cop is the last man she'd fall for. Besides, you just killed your chances, by insinuating that she was a suspect."

"She is. So's your wife."

Ry groaned.

"Maybe you'd rather hire somebody else to conduct this investigation, somebody who'll handle it the way you dictate."

Ry settled his hat over his eyes with a heartfelt sigh. "No. I'll just get used to sleeping down at the bunkhouse until this is cleared up. Freddy has already suggested I might want to take my belongings over there. In fact, I think she suggested I sleep in Romeo's pen." He glanced at Joe. "I've invited our neighbor Eb Whitlock over for dinner tomorrow night so you can get a look at him. Now, there's a suspect worth your time. I know for a fact he wants this place."

"So, we have your top hand, Duane, who needs the ranch as a continued source of employment and a place to raise his experimental herd. We have Belinda, who is fiercely protective of Dexter and wants him to live out his days at the True Love and we have our neighbor, Whitlock. Anybody else?"

Ry managed a smile. "Would you believe a bushy-haired stranger?"

"Nope. Our perpetrator is somebody very close by."

"I'd sure like to convince you that Freddy and Leigh are innocent."

"They'll have to do that for themselves."

"They will. And for the sake of my marriage, I hope it's fast." He started for the door and turned back. "Let me know when you're ready to go down and clean the glass from your car. I'll give you a lift."

"You're not going to con Leigh into doing it?"

Ry grimaced. "After what just happened, I'll be lucky if she agrees to give you a riding lesson tomorrow, even if she's the logical one for the job. Besides, the more you're around her, the sooner you'll eliminate her as a suspect. But to be on the safe side, I'd probably better make up a list of the mean horses. Don't let her put you up on any of those, or you're roadkill."

"Sounds like this will be a challenge."

"That's a slight understatement. Did I mention that these two women are quite . . . independent?"

"You didn't have to. I got the picture the minute I arrived."

Ry shook his head. "All this because of a freak elevator accident. I checked with a few people who know elevators, and that kind of thing almost never happens. With all the safety precautions these days, the odds against it are tremendous. If I didn't know better, I'd say fate had a hand in it."

A shiver rippled down Joe's spine. "I don't believe in fate," he said firmly.

LEIGH KEPT TRACK of Joe's whereabouts for the rest of the day so she wouldn't have to run into him. She wanted to abandon the riding lesson the next morning, too, but the thought of Kyle kept her from doing it. She figured Kyle would be afraid, and she didn't trust Joe to deal sensitively with that fear.

So by breakfast the following morning, she'd resigned herself to spending a few hours in Joe's company. Wanting the experience to get off to a positive start, she approached Joe and Kyle as they ate breakfast in the dining room. She noticed that Kyle had on a *Star Trek* T-shirt today and his Spock ears still poked out under the brim of his Western hat.

"Ready for a ride, cowboy?" she asked him with a reassuring smile.

Kyle looked up from his plate of scrambled eggs, and his blue eyes were troubled. "Hi, Leigh," he said in a subdued voice. "You won't make me go, will you?"

She shot a quick glance at Joe. His expression was tense. "Make you? Of course not."

"If he'd just go down to the corrals with us, I'm sure he'd want to try it," Joe said.

"I don't *like* the corrals, Dad."

"It's the bull you don't like, Kyle," Joe said. "The bull will stay in his pen, right, Leigh?"

"Yes. And Romeo's normally very tame. It's the ropes they tie around him that upset him."

"There, you see?" Joe pushed back his chair. "Let's go check out those horses, buddy."

Kyle's lower lip quivered. "No, Dad. Please."

Joe blew out an exasperated breath. "Kyle—"

"Excuse me, Joe," Leigh interrupted. "Even if Kyle decides to go, I can see he's not quite finished with breakfast. I'd hate to take a cowpoke out on an empty stomach."

Joe opened his mouth to say something, but Leigh barreled on.

"Do you know anything about engines? The truck's making a funny sound. It's parked right out front, so maybe while Kyle finishes his eggs, you could take a look."

Joe gave her a glance of disbelief but he got up from the table. "We'll be back soon, Kyle."

"I really appreciate this," Leigh said as they left the dining room.

"Right." When they reached the deserted front porch, he turned to her. "Now, why don't you tell me why you really brought me out here? I doubt you want me to fix your truck."

"Actually, I do need someone to look at it, although I don't think there's a serious problem. The truck can wait. I got you out here because I have a suggestion about Kyle."

"I am surprised."

Leigh sucked in a breath and prayed for patience. It would be far simpler to hit this man alongside the head with a two-by-four, but tact was required if she intended to protect Kyle. "I agree he needs to get over his fear of the corrals. But I don't think forcing him to go down there is the answer."

"And you do know the answer?"

God, he was maddening. And infuriatingly attractive. His steady gaze had a way of making her forget what she'd been about to say, and the movement of his lips beneath that tantalizing mustache made her want to.... She swallowed and focused on a point beyond his left shoulder. "My Appaloosa mare, Penny Lover, is in foal."

"How nice for her."

"Dammit, will you drop that bored-cop manner of yours for five minutes?"

"What makes you think I can?" he asked quietly.

She stared into the gray depths of his eyes. There had to be a passionate, warm human being hiding behind that granite facade. That was the only explanation for her instinctive need to reach out, no matter how obnoxious he seemed on the surface. "You'd better hope you can," she said. "There's a lot riding on it."

Emotion flickered in his eyes for a second, but was quickly masked.

She soldiered on. "I suggest you take a riding lesson without Kyle so he doesn't feel pressured. When you get back, you can tell him about my mare being due to have a foal soon. Kids are usually fascinated by that. I'll bet Kyle will want to come down and see her himself tomorrow."

"But I want him to learn to ride. We only have six days left."

"Does he have a reason to be afraid of horses?"

"Oh, sure." Joe turned away and propped his hands at his hips while he stared at the mountain-draped horizon. "He has a reason to be afraid of a lot of things, because my ex-wife taught him to be. One of my buddies was a mounted patrolman and he tried to take Kyle up on his horse once. Darlene went ballistic and snatched him down, screaming that he could be killed. He was only three, but I'm sure it made an impression on him."

"Then we need to take it slow. Please don't drag him to the corrals this morning. It would be a miserable experience for all of us."

Joe glanced back at her. "You said yourself I shouldn't abandon him to do my own thing."

"Not for the whole stay, but you can leave him with Belinda and Dexter for a couple of hours. Maybe he'll even miss you and wish he'd gone along."

He hesitated. "I wish I could believe that."

Her heart leapt at this small evidence of a crack in his armor. "Take a risk, Joe," she said. "Believe it." Then she turned and walked into the house. If he'd met her suggestion with an expression of cynicism, she didn't want to see it.

DISAPPOINTMENT OVER Kyle's refusal to come down to the corrals hung over Joe for most of the trip in Leigh's battered truck. But as the weathered fences came into view, Joe's excitement grew. He'd always secretly wanted to be with the mounted unit in New York City, but his superiors had insisted they needed him in the Bronx. As a teenager, he'd ridden a few times in Central Park and had loved it, but once he got on the force, there didn't seem to be any time for hobbies like horseback riding.

After Leigh parked the truck, they got out and started toward the tack shed. She set a brisk pace, her boots thudding rhythmically across the dirt as she called out greetings to the hands who were working on reinforcing the fence in all the places it had been sawed through.

It would be a hot morning's workout. Already Joe's shirt stuck to his back, but physical discomfort had never bothered him much. He took a deep breath, savoring the musky odor of animals and warm earth. "Who are you going to start me on?" he asked. Ry had clued him in as to which horses to avoid, and he wondered if Leigh would try to sneak one of them in, just to humiliate him.

"We'll put you on Mikey."

"Mikey? Isn't he a kid's horse?" Joe realized the hands would be watching this lesson and his pride kicked in. "I think I can handle something a bit more spirited than that."

Leigh gave the brim of her straw cowboy hat a little tug. "Mikey has plenty of spirit, but he's also completely trustworthy. It's a good combination of qualities—for horses and people."

"And extremely rare."

Leigh spun to face him, her eyes dark with fury. "That may be true where you come from, but out here it's the norm," she said in a low voice. "I realize you consider me one of your prime suspects, but you'll have to trust me, at least for the next two hours, or I won't be able to teach you a damn thing."

He gazed at her flushed face, her slightly parted lips, the little drop of moisture that had gathered in the hollow of her throat. She was magnificent. "Well said," he murmured, and tightened his hands into fists to keep from reaching for her.

The fire in her eyes glowed bright for a moment, then gentled into a soft warmth as the corner of her mouth tilted. "Thank you. Now let's get to work."

He helped her carry saddles and bridles to the hitching post. Then he leaned against it while she grabbed two lead ropes and went into the corral after the horses. She moved with assurance through the herd of powerful animals, laying a hand on a muscled shoulder, slapping a shining rump, passing out pieces of carrot, laughing as the animals nuzzled her back pockets for more treats. This was what Joe had wanted Kyle to see, but in a way, he was glad Kyle wasn't here. Joe felt more free to indulge in fantasies that would have seemed inappropriate with his son around.

And Leigh inspired fantasies, with hair the color of honey, a voice shaded with mystery and movements as fluid as a woodland sprite's. She was a seductress in worn denim and scuffed boots. Joe couldn't take his eyes off her.

Finally, she came through the gate leading a bay gelding and a gray mare. All the anger and frustration he'd been so used to seeing in her expression was gone, as if contact with the horses had cleansed her of negative emotions. She held out the lead rope for the gelding. "Here's Mikey."

"I had that one figured out." Joe took the rope and walked Mikey over to the hitching post.

"It doesn't pay to go by names." She tied the gray mare next to Mikey. "We have a mare called Georgina, but mostly we know her as George."

Joe rubbed the white blaze on Mikey's nose. "To confuse the dudes?"

"Well, it does have a way of uncovering the real greenhorns. When someone rides George and says, 'He's a great horse,' we know they didn't check their cinch like they were supposed to. If they had, they'd have noticed that 'he' was missing some necessary equipment." She disappeared into the tack shed, but not before he detected a blush on her cheeks.

When she came back, she had a brush in each hand. She gave him one. "Some of the old cowboys make fun of me for grooming the horses and tell me I'm babying them, but I do it anyway, and I insist the guests do, too." She moved around to the far side of the gray mare, so he could only see her hat. "The horse deserves some pleasure out of the experience," she said.

His groin tightened. All this talk of male equipment and pleasure, combined with the sight of Leigh moving around in snug jeans, was getting to him. "Sounds fair." He concentrated on Mikey's rich mahogany coat that rippled in reaction with each stroke of the brush. Brushing the horse only seemed to enhance the sensuous images assaulting him. He didn't think Leigh was deliberately tormenting him, but maybe she was. Maybe she considered it fit punishment for the suspicions he held about her.

"Be careful around his belly," she warned. "He's ticklish there, just like a lot of people."

"Are you?" He wished the question back immediately.

After a beat of hesitation, she answered, "Sometimes."

He knew if he asked when that was, he was a dead man. He brushed so hard, Mikey stepped sideways and swung his head around as if to ask what maniac was trying to scrub his hide from his body. Joe gentled his motion.

By the time he'd worked his way around to Mikey's right side, Leigh was on the gray mare's left. They worked back to back, and inevitably, as they leaned over, touched backsides. He registered the rounded firmness of her buttocks in that one casual encounter and his mouth went dry. "I think that's good enough," he said, returning to the safety of Mikey's other side.

"Have you ever saddled a horse before?" She sounded slightly out of breath.

"No."

"Then I'll talk you through it." She ducked under Mikey's neck and came to stand next to Joe on Mikey's left side. "The saddle blanket goes first, of course. I'm sure you know that."

"Right." In his present state of mind, he wondered if he would have known anything, including his own name. Somehow, he followed her instructions for positioning the blanket, placing the saddle on Mikey's broad back and drawing in the cinch. But every time her hand accidentally touched his or her breath fell warm on his cheek, he fought the urge to turn and take her in his arms. No matter that there were cowboys all around, or that he needed to maintain his objectivity where this woman was concerned. He was fast becoming obsessed with the need to taste her lips, to feel her body pulled tight against his, to . . .

"You can mount, now."

He stared at her.

"Mikey's ready," she said.

His heart hammered in his chest. "What about you?"

"I'll get you mounted first, and then I'll saddle up."

Of course that's what he'd been referring to. Of course. Like hell. And the color was high on her cheeks. She knew. With shaking hands, he reached for the saddle-horn.

"No." She laid a hand on his arm. A branding iron wouldn't have given off more heat. "If you're going to grab something, take a handful of mane instead."

Oh, he wanted to grab something, all right. He clutched a fistful of Mikey's black mane, shoved his booted foot into the stirrup, and swung up with as much grace as he could muster considering the condition of his swollen manhood.

"Very nice," she said.

He didn't dare look at her. He fumbled with his right foot and managed to slip it into the stirrup on that side.

"The stirrups are too short. Take your feet out and I'll adjust them."

"They feel okay." And he didn't think having her fooling around by his thighs was a good idea at all.

"They're too short. This is western, not English. You're not going to start questioning my judgment at this stage, are you?"

With a small sigh of resignation, he slipped his feet free and eased back on the saddle. But he couldn't ease back far enough to escape the push of her shoulder against his sensitized thighs. He clenched his jaw and tried to think of boring things—traffic duty, paperwork, cold coffee at three in the morning. Nothing erased the sensation of sitting in a warm saddle with all his senses aroused while a bewitching woman stood nudging his inner thigh with her face nearly level with his crotch. She moved to the other side and he held his breath while she puttered with his right stirrup and the denim of his jeans bound him tighter and tighter.

"There." She backed away. "Try that."

*I think you know what I'd like to try,* he thought, thrusting his feet into the stirrups.

"Now stand in them."

Standing was a great suggestion. It relieved some of the pressure.

"Okay. Looking good. Just give me a minute and we'll head over to the round pen."

He needed at least a minute. He wondered if she'd noticed what a state he'd been in, and if she took satisfaction in the way she affected him. Probably yes on both accounts, although he'd been unwilling to meet her gaze and find out. Then there was the flip side of the question—how she was responding to him. If she was toying with him without investing any of herself in the exchange, he could find the courage to turn away. But if she wanted him with even half the intensity he felt . . . He shook his head and swore softly. There would be no escape.

# 5

LEIGH SAT on Pussywillow and watched Joe canter around the aluminum pen they used for training horses and riders. "Keep your heels down," she called. "Grip with your thighs. That's it." A teacher had to keep a close eye on her pupil, she told herself, all the while knowing that images of Joe Gilardini would appear in her dreams tonight. Images this potent always did. His broad shoulders filled out a yoked Western shirt to perfection, and the ripple of powerful thigh muscles beneath his jeans drew her attention more than once. Back in New York, he must have been one tough cop.

He was also a quick study—his lean body had already absorbed the rhythm of the gently loping horse.

"Reverse direction," she called.

His reflexes were lightning fast. She'd known that from the first day when in one economical motion, he'd protected his son from the bull and saved himself. Yet she was amazed at the ease with which he shifted his weight, reined in a tight circle and started off in the other direction. True, he lost a stirrup in the process, but in seconds he had it back. As a teacher, she was gratified. As a woman, she couldn't ignore the sexy tilt of his pelvis as he rocked in the saddle. Her body warmed, remembering how he'd responded to her during the saddling of his horse. But he'd probably choke before he'd acknowledge it. She was a suspect in his investigation, after all. If he was determined not to crack, she wouldn't, either.

He'd only think she was trying to seduce him out of his suspicions, anyway.

A wind had sprung up, swaying the mesquite branches at the edge of the round pen. Rain clouds snagged by the mountains would provide a cooling afternoon deluge, but at ten in the morning, it was still well over a hundred degrees, and Mikey's coat was dark with sweat.

"That's enough work for Mikey this morning," she called. "Slow him to a trot and then we'll take him out on the trail for a little cool down." She rode toward the gate and leaned down to open it. As she fumbled with the latch, a gust of wind blew a bit of dried weed against Pussywillow's foreleg. The mare leapt in fright, and Leigh grabbed a hunk of mane as she started to slide sideways.

"Easy." Joe pulled alongside and clamped a hand on her arm.

She would have been able to right herself, but acting on instinct she allowed him to do it instead. The imprint of his strong fingers burned through the sleeve of her shirt.

"Okay?" he asked, slowly releasing her arm. Very slowly.

She tilted back her hat and gazed at him without speaking for a long moment. Almost independent of their wills, their bodies found excuses to touch and be touched. Perhaps they wouldn't have as much control over this conflagration as she'd thought. "Thanks," she murmured. "I'm fine. Pussywillow's a skittish little mare."

His gaze held hers. "Then why did you choose her to ride?"

"She has a wonderfully soft mouth."

Joe's gray eyes darkened and his glance drifted to
Leigh's mouth. Then, as if catching himself, he turned
away. "Let's go," he muttered, wheeling Mikey around.

Shaken, Leigh led the way out of the round pen. This
was getting too heavy. She should definitely lighten up.
She would advise Joe to do the same, but she didn't think
it was in his nature.

She decided to take him out to the site of the old
homestead. The trail there was fairly level and wide
enough to ride two abreast, so she could keep an eye on
his technique. At least that was the excuse she gave herself for watching how he moved in the saddle. "You're
doing well, but you could ease up on the reins a little,"
she said.

He relaxed the reins a fraction. "Thanks."

"How does it feel?"

Unexpectedly, he flashed her a smile. "Great."

The smile caught her like a blow to the stomach. God
but he was attractive when he did that. His mustache
gave his smile a rakish look that took her breath away,
and for the first time, she contemplated the enormous
appeal of Joe Gilardini having fun.

For the next few minutes they rode in a silence broken
only by the call of quail and the chatter of cactus wrens.
Yet the atmosphere felt anything but peaceful to Leigh,
as her sensitized awareness recorded the rhythm of Joe's
breathing, the slightest movement of his hands, the direction of his gaze. She even imagined she could hear his
heart beat. When he let out a satisfied sigh, she felt as if
the air had been pushed from her own lungs.

"I don't understand what could be scary about all
this," he said. "When I was a kid, I would have given
anything to ride a horse and be a cowboy."

"Seems like the kid grew up to do exactly that."

He gave her a wry smile. "I guess you're right. And I thought that Kyle would be as excited about it as I am."

"Give him time."

Joe sighed again. "Time. I can't believe he's already seven. If I don't connect with him soon, it's going to be too late."

"I'll tell you a secret. Out here, time isn't something to be bludgeoned into submission the way it is back in New York."

"Is that so?"

"Ask Ry McGuinnes if you don't believe me. When I first met Ry, he was hell-bent-for-leather, just like you. Wanted me to teach him riding the first day, team roping the second. That's an Easterner's way of attacking life, trying to cram too many things into each hour. Ry's beginning to understand that most worthwhile things can't be accomplished that way."

"I've never been real long on patience, myself."

Leigh nodded. "That's okay. You've come to the right place for learning some." She pulled Pussywillow to a halt as they entered a clearing. On the far side, a cracked concrete rectangle and a few scattered pieces of adobe were all that was left of the homestead.

Joe leaned on his saddlehorn and looked around. "So this is the site of the stampede that almost killed Freddy and Ry."

"This is where everything began, when Thaddeus Singleton built the homestead, brick by brick, back in 1882."

Joe swung down from the saddle. "I want to look around. Should I tie him somewhere?"

"Just drop the reins to the ground. Mikey will stay put. Unless there's another stampede." Leigh dismounted and tethered Pussywillow to a nearby mesquite before she walked over toward Joe.

He turned. "Think there will be another stampede?"

She paused and met his gaze. "If you're implying I lured you out here to cause some accident to befall you, then come right out and say so, Officer."

"No, I don't really think that." He walked over to the cracked concrete and gazed at it. A gray green lizard about eight inches long scurried across the surface, paused for a few lizard push-ups and scuttled away into the desert beyond the slab.

"This concrete hasn't been here since 1882," Joe observed.

"The concrete was poured in the thirties to help stabilize the house. Even though no one had lived in it for several years, the hands still used it as a place to get out of the sun or the rain. But by the sixties there was no roof to speak of, so it was abandoned to the elements."

Joe wandered the perimeter of the ruin. "Why did Thaddeus pick this spot?"

"Supposedly because there wasn't as much caliche here, and his wife Clara wanted a small garden. Dexter told me that. Clara didn't die until a few years after Dexter and Belinda came to work at the ranch, so they both knew her."

"What's caliche?"

"Layers of mineral deposits hard as granite. I've seen my dad take a stick of dynamite to make a hole through it so he could plant a tree."

Joe stood, his hands in his back pockets, and gazed around him. "Why wasn't the next ranch house built here, then?"

"Privacy, I suppose. The son and daughter-in-law probably wanted some distance between themselves and the old folks. But Clara hung on to this place as long as she could, I'm told, even without plumbing and electricity. My grandfather said she cried when she was forced to move into the big house. I guess I can understand it."

"I'm sure you can." His gray eyes were assessing. "But I expect you'd do something more active than cry if you were put in the same position."

"I am in the same position, as you very well know."

"What if I said, right now, that I don't want the True Love sold to developers," he said quietly. "Would the sabotage stop?"

She matched him, squint for squint. "I have no idea." She hesitated, but the question was too important not to ask it. "Now that you've seen some of the area, how do you feel about the sale of the ranch?"

"I have no idea."

Frustration made her spin away from him and stare up at the mountains towering above them. "What colossal arrogance! The True Love has been nurturing families for over a hundred years, yet here you come, some city slicker from New York, and imagine you have the right to snap your fingers and relegate it to the bulldozers, all because you hold the almighty purse strings! I find that kind of irreverence incomprehensible." She took a deep breath, knowing she had to cool it. She was already a prime suspect. An emotional outburst would tighten the noose around her neck.

Joe remained silent for several moments, as if allowing her to collect herself. "Well, at least we've established one thing."

She turned back. "We have?"

"You're not going to try and sweet-talk me into deciding to keep the ranch."

She watched the flicker of amusement in his eyes. A sheepish smile made its way through her anger. "Guess not."

"That's a shame."

Her heart, slowed from its angry pounding of a minute ago, began to beat to a brighter rhythm. "It is? Why?"

Joe's mouth curved. "There's a good chance you could have done it." Turning away, he walked toward his horse and swung himself into the saddle.

JOE NOTICED that Leigh didn't have much to say on the ride back. He helped her brush the horses and turn them into the corral, and all the while aware that she kept sneaking looks at him. Maybe she was regretting not trying to seduce him. Inadvertently she almost had, but he vowed she'd never know how close he came to pulling her into his arms at the homestead site. Her passionate defense of the ranch had colored her cheeks and lit dark flames in her eyes, making her nearly irresistible. But he did resist. She was too loyal to her ancestral home to be dismissed as a suspect. At the end of this investigation, someone would go to jail, and that someone could still be Leigh.

"If you're up to it, we can go out again tomorrow and see more of the ranch," she said as they drove back to the ranch house.

"That pond in Rogue Canyon sounds like a great place to take Kyle," he said. "If there are some poles around, we might do a little fishing."

"I can find you some poles, but I wouldn't set my heart on taking Kyle up there yet. He'd have to ride a horse, and I'm not sure he'll agree to it so soon. Just getting him down to the corrals will be a victory."

"We'll see." Joe wondered if she really thought Kyle wouldn't want to come, or if she wanted another crack at being alone with him now that he'd admitted his vulnerability to her charms. Joe was determined to take Kyle on that ride the next day. His son would be the perfect chaperon.

When they arrived at the ranch house, he reached for the door handle on the truck. "Thanks for the riding lesson," he said as he climbed down. "In exchange, I'll check that funny noise in the engine. Could be just a speck of dust in the carburetor."

"That's okay," she said quickly, hopping to the dirt. "Duane can look at it later."

"But I can look at it now." He snared her with a glance across the truck's dark blue hood. "Sort of even things up between us."

"What's the matter? Are you afraid to be indebted to me?"

"Maybe."

She tossed him the keys. "You do make things tough on yourself, Officer. You can bring these back to me when you come in for lunch. And thanks."

"Anytime." The little unicorn's horn bit into his palm as he caught the keys. He watched her walk away without a backward glance, her hourglass figure beckoning him with every step. At first he'd thought she didn't want him nosing around her truck, but then she'd let him have the keys with such nonchalance he decided he'd been wrong.

After opening the hood, he started the truck and took off the air filter. He used his handkerchief to clean the butterfly valve on the carburetor and the hesitation in the engine seemed to go away. The whole procedure had taken less than five minutes, so he left the truck running and climbed back into the cab. The glove compartment contained the usual ownership and insurance papers, a few colored stones and a worn copy of a book called *Creative Visualizations* by somebody named Shakti Gawain. He sniffed the book. It smelled vaguely of incense, of mystery, of secrets. As he opened it, he felt that he was peering into the fascinating labyrinth of Leigh's mind.

Glancing around to make sure no one noticed, he flipped through the book and read a few underlined passages. They spoke of going with the flow and not forcing issues, letting life unfold. Joe shook his head. Damned passive philosophy as far as he was concerned. It also didn't fit with the type of person who would commit sabotage. He closed the book and put it back in the glove compartment, arranging everything as he'd found it. Then he turned off the engine and pocketed the keys, unicorn and all.

As he walked in the front door of the ranch house, the hum of voices from the dining room told him lunch was already in progress. He ducked into his room to wash up and noticed Kyle's backpack lying open on his bed, his Star Trek figures strewn about. The kid had apparently spent some time in the room by himself playing with the plastic toys when he could have been in the fresh air learning a new skill. Well, Joe would see that didn't happen two days in a row.

When he reached the arched entry to the dining room, he noticed Kyle and Leigh sitting together at a table. Kyle's fair head so close to Leigh's honey-colored one made them look remarkably like mother and son. Had Kyle really been Leigh's, he wouldn't be so lacking in courage, Joe thought. Leigh had the heart of a lioness.

She spotted him and spoke to Kyle, who swiveled in his chair and waved wildly.

"Over here, Dad!"

He strode over, determined to convince Kyle to go fishing with him the next day. There had to be some significant change in the way this vacation was going.

"Did you know Leigh's horse is going to have a baby?" Kyle said before Joe could form the first part of his argument.

"Yes, I did, and I think—"

"I'm going down there with you guys tomorrow morning," Kyle said. "I want to see that mother horse. Leigh said the baby could be born *any day*."

Joe glanced at Leigh, who looked somewhat wise and smug, but then she had a right to, he supposed. He opened his mouth to tack on a suggestion for the fishing trip, but the exhortations from Leigh's book drifted through his mind. Not that he believed in that stuff, but maybe this time he wouldn't push for more just yet. He'd stick the fishing poles in the back of the truck, just in case, though.

"When you checked the truck, did you find anything?" Leigh asked.

He blinked, giving away far too much information for someone of Leigh's perceptive abilities. "It was probably dust in the carburetor," he said, digging her keys out of his pocket. "Seems okay now."

"Thank you for investigating."

He was sure she knew exactly what he'd been up to, poking around through her glove compartment, looking for anything that would shed light on the strange occurrences at the ranch. She was either innocent or very smart. Then there was the outside possibility she was both.

He turned to Kyle. "I'm going to pound the dents out of the car this afternoon. Want to help me?"

"Dexter and me, we were gonna play Junior Scrabble." Kyle looked worried, as if he suspected this might not be the right response.

Joe swallowed his disappointment and sat down at the table with a determined smile. Go with the flow. "No problem, Kyle. What's for lunch?"

THE AFTERNOON rain played havoc with Joe's plan to pound the dents out of his car. He'd never seen a storm come on so fast. He barely had time to cover the broken window with a tarp before it hit, sluicing down as if from a giant bucket. Carrying his tools, he ran for cover under the front porch, only to watch his tarp blow away from the window and the rain pour in, drenching his seat covers. Then, as quickly as the storm swept in, it departed. Determined to finish the job, Joe trudged back out and worked in the mud for another half hour before the storm, growling like an angry dog, turned and headed back at him. This time, instead of running for cover, he continued to work as rain dripped from his hair, eyebrows and nose.

Pounding furiously on the caved-in steel, he didn't hear anyone approach until Leigh yelled in his ear. He dropped the mallet in the ooze at his feet and whirled, his hand automatically going for his weaponless hip.

She leapt back and nearly fell in the muck. He grabbed her just in time, his fingers slipping, then tightening on the yellow raincoat she was wearing.

"You crazy idiot!" She shook away his grasp and adjusted her floppy yellow rain hat.

With her hair in a braid down her back and her rain boots peeking out from under her coat, she looked about twelve years old. He smiled in spite of himself. "A *grin-ning* idiot, no less! Don't you hear that thunder? You could be struck by lightning out here!"

Apparently, she'd donned rain gear to come out in the thunderstorm to warn him. Probably for Kyle's sake, he thought sullenly.

"I'm almost done!" he yelled back. "Five more minutes, tops!"

She grabbed him by the shoulders and tried to shake him, but she didn't make much headway. "Didn't you hear me? You could get hit!" A flash followed by an explosion of sound sharp as the crack of a rifle punctuated her statement. "Come inside this minute!"

The next flash nearly blinded him, and instinctively he grabbed her and pulled them both through the open door of the car onto the soggy driver's seat as the crash made him temporarily deaf. When he could hear again, he realized his elbow was on the horn. Leigh was wedged on top of him as they sprawled half in, half out of the car. He didn't think the bolt had struck the Cavalier, but if it had, at least the tires would have grounded them.

He moved his elbow and the horn stopped its blaring. The rain, too, seemed to lessen at the same moment. He looked into Leigh's eyes, wide with shock. Her rain hat was gone, knocked into the mud at their feet, most likely.

"You're right," he murmured. "It's dangerous out here."

She opened her mouth, but no words came out, and she closed it again. She was so close, he could count each individual rain-damp eyelash and admire the subtle shades of gold and brown in her eyes. He watched her pupils widen with awareness as he cradled the back of her head and brought her the last two inches necessary to mold her lips to his.

With that velvet touch, he forgot the gearshift jabbing his right side and the rain soaking his jeans. He forgot that he should keep his distance from this woman who could be guilty of sabotage, who might monopolize his son, who might jeopardize his sanity with her crazy view of the world. There was only the soft, moist temptation of full lips that tasted of some exotic spice that his fevered brain couldn't identify. But he wanted more. Much more. With a groan, he pressed deeper and she opened like a tropical flower in the heat of the jungle. He dipped his tongue inside her mouth and grew drunk with the pleasure he received there. Nothing mattered but this. So rich, so lush, so—

"What's the deal, here?" boomed a voice from outside the car. "Leigh, what're you doing hanging half-out of that heap of tin? You two look like a couple of sardines that refused to be canned!" The last was followed by a bark of laughter.

Leigh struggled out of Joe's arms, and he let her go. Whoever the bastard was who'd ended that kiss would pay for it one day, Joe vowed.

"Well, hello, Eb," Leigh said with a show of dignity that impressed Joe no end. She stood beside the car and straightened her raincoat. She offered no explanation, either, which Joe liked even more. "Ry and Freddy told me you were coming for dinner. I'd like you to meet Joe Gilardini."

Joe hauled himself out of the car and held out his hand to Eb Whitlock, one of Ry's prime suspects. He was a large man, dressed dramatically in a black shirt with silver embroidery on the yoke. A heavy silver and turquoise bolo tie hung around his neck and an equally large and expensive-looking buckle graced his expansive belly.

Joe could understand why Ry wanted this guy to be the saboteur. There was a lot to dislike about Eb Whitlock.

"The third partner." Eb flashed a set of large teeth and gave Joe a bone-crushing handshake. Joe crushed right back and had the satisfaction of seeing Eb wince. Eb retrieved his hand and adjusted his bolo tie, while managing to show off a silver and turquoise watchband at the same time. "I understand you're a cop."

"Was," Joe said. "Now I'm just a private citizen, like the rest of you."

Eb gestured toward the Cavalier. "Must not have paid you much."

"I got by."

"Come on into the house, Eb," Leigh said, starting toward the flagstone walk, shiny with rain. "Dinner will be in a half hour, Joe," she said over her shoulder.

"I'll be there." He would cherish every minute of putting Whitlock on the hot seat.

Leigh glanced at Eb as they started up the walk. "I was just having some Bengal Spice tea with honey. You're welcome to join me."

*Bengal Spice with honey,* Joe thought. So that was the exotic taste that had captivated him so. Except he wasn't sure it was entirely the tea she'd been drinking that had made her so inviting.

"You and your herb tea," Eb said, putting an arm around Leigh's shoulders. "Got any good Scotch?"

Joe clenched his fists. One kiss gave him no rights. No rights whatsoever. Just before they stepped up on the porch, the sun burst out from behind a cloud and splashed the yard, making the potted geraniums glow with passion. A stray sunbeam reached up and fingered a tendril of Leigh's hair that had escaped from the braid. Something about seeing the sun in her hair made his throat hurt. He leaned down and picked up the yellow rain hat and carefully brushed away the mud.

# 6

As Leigh took off her muddy boots on the porch and shook out her raincoat, she kept up a normal conversation with Eb Whitlock about the number of inches of rain they'd had so far this season. Yet nothing would ever be normal again. She could still sense the power behind the lightning strike, still feel the electricity singing through the air, sizzling against her lips, igniting a passion that would never sleep again. The drumming of the rain on the car roof had echoed the drumming of her heart as he'd closed the gap between them....

"If you were smart, you'd have that cop investigate all the little accidents you've had around here," Eb said as he held the carved wooden door open for her.

Leigh pulled her thoughts together with difficulty and gave the response she and Ry had agreed upon. "Joe's on vacation while he's out here. All he wants to do is relax. In fact, tomorrow I'm taking him up to the pond for a little bass fishing."

"Sounds like fiddlin' while Rome burns, if you ask me." Eb followed her into the main room of the ranch house. "Don't tell me you're not hurting for business. How many guests you got right now?"

"Five. But it's usually slow in August. Sit down, Eb," she said with thinly disguised irritation as she waved him toward an overstuffed leather chair. "I'll order us something to drink."

"I'll take a glass of ginger ale," Freddy said, coming out of her office. "How are you, Eb? Hope the drive over didn't get that new truck of yours too muddy."

"A truck like mine's built to take a little mud. Just last week I drove it across the riverbed after some strays, and it didn't get stuck once. They don't make them any better than that model."

Leigh hurried from the room before she had to hear another story about Eb's marvelous truck. She might have been more tolerant if Eb had earned the money to finance his materialistic tastes, but his wife had inherited the tidy sum that had allowed Eb to buy a hundred acres from Leigh's father twenty-five years ago. When Loraine Whitlock died, Eb seemed to focus completely on his possessions and made no bones about wanting to add the True Love to his list of things to brag about.

She found Manny, one of two waiters they kept on in the summer months, arranging place settings in the dining room. She gave him the drinks order and he nodded.

"Thanks, Manny," she said. "Maybe you'd better bring a beer for Ry, too. He should show up soon. Make that two beers," she added. "I imagine Joe Gilardini will be joining us, too."

Manny grinned. "That little kid of his has been playing Scrabble all afternoon with Dex. Belinda loves it, because Dex is using words he couldn't remember before. The kid taught them how to do high fives, and every time Dexter uses a new word, there are high fives all around. You should see Belinda and Dexter doing a high five. It's hilarious."

Leigh's chuckle was tinged with admiration. "Kyle's a great kid." If only Joe could appreciate his son's strengths instead of focusing on his weaknesses, she thought sadly. She thanked Manny again and returned to the living room, where Ry had joined the group. Down the hall, the door to Joe's room was closed. She suspected he was inside cleaning up. Taking off his clothes. Taking a shower.

With an effort, she pushed those thoughts aside and smiled at Ry and Freddy, who had apparently settled their differences and were tucked into the love seat with Ry's arm draped possessively over the leather back.

Eb glanced at Leigh as she chose a seat on the long sofa. "I've just been telling Ry and Freddy what I told you, Leigh. You folks can't go on this way. Admit it, your bookings are down for the fall season."

"The rodeo will generate more business," Freddy said. She paused as Manny came in and served the drinks. "Once we have the arena set up, we can schedule another rodeo in November and perhaps even a third in February. Amanda has some dynamite ideas for promotion. We'll be okay."

Ry picked up his bottle of beer and took a swallow. "And speaking of the rodeo, Eb, we'd like to rent Grateful Dead for the bull-riding competition."

Freddy almost spilled her ginger ale as her glance snapped toward her husband. "And who, pray tell, plans to ride that monster? Don't tell me. I think I can guess." Putting down her glass, she stood and walked over to the fireplace, where she turned back to face Ry. "I'd hoped Romeo had knocked some sense into that thick skull of yours."

Ry shrugged. "I rode him."

Freddy threw up her hands in a gesture of frustration. "I give up. My baby's destined to be the child of a cripple."

"Baby?" asked Joe, who walked in just in time for Freddy's last statement. His hair still damp and curled from the shower, and attired in a fresh Western shirt and jeans, he made Leigh catch her breath. His gaze rested warmly on her for a brief second before he turned to Freddy. "What's this about a baby?"

"We're going to have one." She paused to glare at her husband. "Although I'm beginning to think men as hardheaded as Ry McGuinnes shouldn't be allowed to reproduce."

Joe grinned and addressed Ry. "Congratulations." His gaze swept to include Freddy. "That's great news . . . isn't it?"

Freddy gestured toward Ry. "Go ahead. Tell him what a fool you are."

Ry reached for the extra beer on the coffee table and handed it to Joe. "Eb here has a Brahma bull that's never been ridden to the buzzer."

"And why you keep him I'll never know," Freddy put in.

"Because he's the best," Eb said with a Chesire-cat smile. "I get offers from rodeo stock people all the time who want to buy him outright, but I'm not selling. If you want to try ridin' him, McGuinnes, be my guest. I might even waive the rental fee, seeing as how we're neighbors."

"How charitable of you," Leigh murmured. Eb would love to see Ry knocked six ways to Sunday. A disabled Ry would improve the rancher's chances for acquiring the True Love. "I agree with Freddy, Ry," Leigh said. "That bull is a tough customer. Romeo is a sweetheart unless you put the bull rope on him, but Grateful Dead is another story."

Eb laughed and glanced at Joe. "Know why he's called Grateful Dead? Because after he tosses you, you're grateful you ain't dead."

"Nobody can deny he'd be a great draw for the rodeo," Ry said, taking another swig of his beer.

"The Christians and the lions were a great draw for the Roman-coliseum crowd, too," Freddy said. "I never figured you for a martyr, though."

"I've decided you're all martyrs," Eb said. "Flying in the face of the True Love Curse."

"And what is that, again?" Joe asked. "I never can get these superstitions straight."

"The cavalry massacred some Indians on this land, so the Indians cursed it and said no white man would ever make a profit here," Eb said.

"Is that so?" Joe gazed at Eb. "Then why are you—" He stopped speaking as Kyle ran into the room.

Kyle skidded to a stop and glanced uncertainly at his father. "Belinda told me to wash up for dinner."

"Who's this?" Eb boomed, leaning over the arm of his chair to stare at Kyle. "And what're those funny things on his ears?"

Joe walked over to Kyle and placed a hand on the boy's shoulder. "This is my son, Kyle," he said in an even tone. "Kyle, this is Mr. Whitlock, who owns the Rocking W Ranch right next to ours. I guess he's not a 'Star Trek' fan."

Eb blinked. "'Star Trek'? Oh, I see. That weird guy with the ears, Dr. Spock or something."

Kyle drew himself up straighter. "*Mr.* Spock," he said.

Ry joined the exchange, a challenging gleam in his eye. "You have to forgive Mr. Whitlock, Kyle. At his age, it's tough to keep up with things."

"Now, wait a minute," blustered Eb. "I never wanted to keep up with all that space stuff."

"Exactly Ry's point," Leigh said. "Space is the wave of the future, a concept for the younger generation."

Kyle's gaze swung from Ry to Leigh. Leigh winked at him and a slow smile spread across his face.

"Better go wash up, buddy," Joe said, squeezing Kyle's shoulder gently.

"Okay." Kyle turned to Eb with new confidence. "Nice meeting you. I'm sorry you're so old."

Leigh bit the inside of her lip to keep from laughing as Kyle skipped from the room. A glance into Joe's twinkling eyes told her he'd enjoyed the interchange as much as she had. And he'd acknowledged his son, Spock ears and all. She raised her tea mug slightly in salute. He responded with an almost imperceptible lift of his beer bottle and his teeth flashed beneath his mustache in a brief smile. Leigh felt giddy with hope, and the beginnings of a deeper emotion she dared not give a name to.

ALL JOE WANTED was five minutes alone with Leigh to apologize. Wonderful though the kiss had been, it never should have happened. He'd put her at risk. He'd been so determined to finish the damn car door that he'd ignored his own safety, which wasn't too smart, considering his responsibility to Kyle. He hated to think he'd developed such a taste for personal danger over the years that he'd welcome a lightning storm.

But regardless of his own stupidity, he'd almost caused injury to Leigh. He hoped she'd forgive him, although he doubted he'd ever forgive himself.

The dinner with Eb Whitlock dragged on forever, it seemed. When the festivities moved from the dining room to the living room, Joe excused himself to put Kyle to bed. When he returned, Eb was back in the over-stuffed chair he seemed to prefer, drinking coffee with Leigh, Freddy and Ry. Two of the guests, a couple from

Japan, had joined the group and seemed entranced by Eb's stories.

Joe stood in front of the fireplace and observed Eb. No doubt the guy was acquisitive, not to mention obnoxious, but Joe had a hard time imagining he'd stage all the accidents just to add another hundred and sixty acres to his holdings. The bragging value didn't seem high enough for that, and owning the True Love wouldn't change Eb's life appreciably. Time and again Joe had to consider who had the most at stake—Belinda, Duane, Freddy. . . and Leigh. Under normal circumstances none of them would react this way, but he, Ry and Chase had backed them into a corner, and that could produce dangerous behavior.

When Eb finally left, Ry cornered Joe and indicated he wanted a powwow on the patio. Joe spent a half hour explaining to a very disappointed Ry that he didn't think Eb was the culprit.

"You said yourself these were desperate acts," Joe said as they sat in lounge chairs. The pool, lit from beneath the water, glowed in its tiled setting like a smooth turquoise. The rain had cooled the night air until it was almost crisp, and no evening swimmers marred the glasslike surface.

"The brushfire was definitely the act of a desperate person," Ry said. "And I might add that my wife was nowhere near the ranch when it broke out."

Joe waved aside the comment. "People can be hired. She could be in league with Belinda, Dexter or Leigh. My point is, all of those people have reasons to be desperate. Whitlock doesn't. I can see why you'd like to nail him. He's an irritating son of a bitch, but unfortunately that's not against the law."

"You sound like Lavette. He keeps telling me not to let my dislike of Whitlock get in the way of my judgment. But I keep thinking there might be something we don't know, something that would make Whitlock willing to commit those acts. I think he's vicious enough. He can hardly wait to get me on that bull of his."

"Yeah, what's that all about? Do you have a death wish or something?"

Ry grinned. "That bull will probably toss me six ways to Sunday, but having him perform will be good publicity for the rodeo, and I'm about the only guy willing to get aboard. And who knows? Maybe by some miracle I'll stay on for eight seconds. It would be sweet if I could make it to the buzzer and wipe that damned smirk off Whitlock's mug. But all of that's secondary, really."

"And what's primary?"

"The real reason I'm riding that bull is that I can't ever let Freddy think she's tamed me. She's a hell of a strong woman, and once I start saying, 'Yes, dear,' our relationship will go downhill fast. I have to keep that balance."

Joe laughed and shook his head. "Watching you two is sort of like watching King Kong and Godzilla battle it out."

"I wouldn't let Freddy hear you say that. I doubt she'd feel flattered to be compared to either of those characters, especially after she starts getting a little rounder, if you know what I mean." Ry pushed himself up from the chair. "Well, I can see you're not going to support my case against Whitlock, so I'd better go find that wife of mine and see if she'll welcome me into her bed tonight. It's never a sure thing."

"Sounds like a rough way to live."

"Nah. I love a challenge." Ry adjusted his hat and walked inside.

After he left, Joe went looking for Leigh. She wasn't in the living room or dining room. When he poked his head in through the swinging door of the kitchen, Belinda looked up from the table where she was busy making out a shopping list.

"Still hungry, cowboy?" she said in her lilting voice.

He liked being called that. "No, thanks. Dinner was great. Have you seen Leigh?"

Belinda's eyes twinkled. "Try the front porch. She likes to sit out there with Dexter and Chloe."

As Belinda had predicted, Joe found Dexter and Leigh sitting in the shadows with Dexter's black-and-white dog curled at their feet. Dexter said something in a low voice and Leigh laughed softly. Joe's heart turned over at the inviting sound of it.

The dog noticed him first and raised her head.

Then Leigh glanced toward the door, her delicate silver earrings winking in the light spilling from a nearby window. She'd combed her hair free of its braid and it hung free down her back. "Hello, Joe."

The sound of his name coming from her lips was sweet torture. "Hi."

"Dexter was telling me about the Scrabble game with Kyle. I guess they had a great afternoon together."

"Great," Dexter echoed.

"Glad to hear it." Joe wondered how to describe his afternoon. Earth-shattering, perhaps.

The front door opened behind him and Belinda stepped out. "Bedtime, Dexter," she said.

"You're sure?" Dexter asked.

"I'm sure," she replied firmly.

"Okay." Dexter reached for his walker. "Come on, dog. What's her name, again?"

"Chloe," Leigh said.

"Chloe," Dexter repeated. "Why can't I remember?"

"You will," Leigh said gently. "Every day you're getting better, Dex. Keep playing Scrabble with Kyle."

"Great game," Dexter said as he pulled himself erect and moved the walker across the wooden porch toward his wife. "High fives."

"Kyle was so sweet to play with Dexter all afternoon," Belinda said to Joe. "He's a nice boy."

"I'm sure he enjoyed it, too," Joe said.

"I hope so. Good night, you two."

"Good night," Leigh and Joe said together.

Joe held the door for them as they went inside, Belinda following Dexter's measured progress and Chloe trotting behind Belinda. Then he quietly closed the door.

"Kyle accomplished quite a feat this afternoon," Leigh said.

"What's that?" So aware of her that his skin tingled, he sat on the chair recently vacated by Dexter.

"With that Scrabble game, he's found a teaching tool that might help Dexter overcome some of his communication difficulties. And a boy with an empathetic personality like Kyle's is perfect for working with Dexter."

"That's great, of course, but—" He paused, knowing they were dealing with thorny issues, wishing he could just sit here and absorb the magic of the night a little longer.

"But?"

"Kyle spends too much time indoors, as it is. I was hoping this vacation would be different for him."

A tense silence followed his comment. "There are times when it's prudent to be indoors," she said at last.

So she regretted the moment they'd shared, he thought with a sinking sensation in his stomach. "You're right. That's why I came out here, to apologize for this afternoon. I should never have—"

"Kissed me?" The question had a harsh ring.

"That's—"

"I'm sure you regret giving in to your impulses." She stood and walked to the edge of the porch. "A good lawman doesn't let emotion interfere with his judgment like that, does he? And certainly not with the suspect in a crime."

He ran his finger thoughtfully over his mustache as he gazed at her profile, cold and unyielding in the pale light from the stars. "No, I wasn't acting very professionally this afternoon," he said.

She crossed her arms and looked up at the night sky, free of clouds now, although there was no moon. "I'm guessing you're a Scorpio."

"Which, I suppose, explains everything."

"It explains a lot." She didn't even gloat over the fact she'd been right about his sign.

"Don't try to pin labels on me, Leigh."

She turned back to him, her face shadowed. "Not labels. Human traits. Human frailties. You do have them."

He pushed out of the chair and stepped closer. "I realize that. I just said I made some mistakes this afternoon."

"Mistakes you plan to correct, I take it."

A soft breeze carried her wildflower scent to him. His heart pounded as desire stalked him like a jungle cat. "You tell me. You have all the answers."

"So do you." Her voice caressed the air around him. "You just don't realize it."

"Probably not. I'm not as subtle as you." Need tightened his chest, making breathing a chore.

"Ah. It's not a big step from subtle to devious, now, is it?"

"Stop it, Leigh. I didn't say that."

"But I expect you were thinking it. How inconvenient for a man of your sensibilities that you're attracted to someone who could turn out to be your criminal." She leaned against a post and wrapped her arms behind it in a provocative gesture that lifted and defined her breasts beneath the soft material of her blouse. "I should take pity on you and keep out of your way, I suppose. But it's too much fun trying to get a rise out of you, so to speak."

He lost the battle. Muttering an oath, he slid one hand behind the small of her back and the other behind the nape of her neck. He took some small satisfaction in the knowledge that she was trembling.

"My goodness." Her voice was raspy, which excited him all the more. "Are we about to be unprofessional again?"

"You witch." He pulled her roughly against him and took her mouth in a kiss meant to punish. Yet when she opened to him, the lush promise of her lips drowned his anger and replaced it with blinding passion. All of her teasing dissolved into the most honest response he'd ever experienced from a woman. She held nothing back, and in seconds he was fully, achingly aroused.

Yet now was not the time to finish this. Maybe the time would never come. Steeling himself for deprivation, he released her and backed away.

She leaned against the post again, her chest heaving. Then she ran her tongue slowly over her lips, and he groaned. "Coward," she whispered. He turned away, not trusting himself to reply to her taunt.

"Sleep well, cowboy," she murmured.

He heard her move from the post and walk across the porch to the front door. When at last it closed behind her, he let out a long, shaky breath. Sleep well. What a laugh.

# 7

LEIGH WAS DETERMINED that the trip to the corrals the next morning would be a good experience for Kyle. If Joe wasn't satisfied with the way everything turned out, that was too damn bad. Joe needed an attitude adjustment, and she was just the woman to give him one.

All three of them rode down in her truck with Kyle sitting between Leigh and Joe. She'd located a couple of fishing poles and lures that Chase Lavette had used on his last expedition to the pond, and Belinda had packed them all a lunch, just in case Kyle agreed to the trail ride. But Joe would not force the issue. Not on her watch, she'd decided.

"Do you think Penny Lover could have her baby *today*?" Kyle asked as the truck bounced along the road, rattling the fishing poles in the back.

"I don't know," Leigh said. "After I check her this morning, I'll be able to tell you."

"I wish she would. I've never seen a real baby horse before." Kyle looked up at Joe. "Have you, Dad?"

"Just in the movies," Joe said.

"They're pretty cute," Leigh said, "trying to stand on those wobbly legs, their stubby little tails wiggling around for balance. As far as I'm concerned, the birth of a foal is the most exciting thing that happens on the True Love."

"I think so, too," Kyle said, his voice full of reverence. As they reached the corrals and Leigh stopped the truck, he scrambled to his knees, digging the toe of his boot into her thigh in the process. "Which one is she?"

"You can't see her too well from here. I have her in one of the far corrals by herself." She opened her door. "Ready?"

"Yep."

Leigh smiled to herself. The afternoon spent with Dexter had made an impression. Kyle was beginning to sound like a cowboy. Except for the Spock ears, he looked like any other little boy who'd grown up on a ranch, with his red plaid Western shirt and a belt cinching his jeans tight so they wouldn't slide down over his skinny hips. But when his booted feet hit the ground, his city roots became obvious. A ranch boy would have taken off running for the corrals. Kyle looked over at the milling herd of horses, which looked more imposing now that he was out of the truck. He shrank back and grabbed Leigh's hand.

She wished he'd grabbed Joe's hand instead. Joe had his stoic mask in place, as if he hadn't noticed Kyle's gesture, but she'd bet money he had, and was hurt by it. The day Joe Gilardini surrendered completely to his human emotions would be a glorious one indeed. Leigh wondered if she'd be around to see it.

Leigh gave Kyle's hand a reassuring squeeze. "Let's go see Penny Lover."

Kyle nodded, too overwhelmed by his surroundings to speak.

When they neared the corral, the Appaloosa spotted Leigh and shoved her nose over the fence. Leigh fed her a carrot from her pocket and scratched behind the horse's ear. "How's my little mother today? I brought you some visitors."

"All I can see is her head," Kyle complained.

Leigh had anticipated that Kyle wouldn't be able to see over the solid mesquite fence, but she'd decided against picking him up. Like any young animal, he needed to start learning how to get around on his own.

"Here's how you climb up, Kyle." She demonstrated by placing her foot in a crevice and pulling herself up.

Kyle looked at her doubtfully. "I might fall."

"Not if you choose your footholds carefully. You can do it."

Kyle took a deep breath and stepped up to the fence. His progress was slow, but Leigh resisted the urge to help. At one point, she glanced at Joe. He returned her glance and mouthed the word *thanks*. She felt inordinately pleased with herself.

Kyle reached the top and peered over. "Wow, she's *fat*."

Leigh and Joe laughed, and Penny Lover tossed her head.

"She won't be fat much longer," Leigh said. Unlatching the gate, she slipped inside the corral, another piece of carrot handy to calm the horse. "Easy, girl. She's a Blanket-hip Appaloosa," she explained as she stroked Penny Lover's swollen belly. "That means the front part of her is solid, in this case brown, and her rump and hips are flecked with white."

"Will her baby look like that?" Kyle asked.

"I sure hope so. That's the gamble. We never know if the offspring will carry the Appaloosa markings or not." She took another piece of carrot from her jeans pocket and walked toward Kyle. Penny Lover followed. "Want to give her a piece of carrot?"

Fear and yearning vied in his blue gaze.

"She won't bite you. Just hold your hand flat and she'll take the carrot off with her lips."

Slowly Kyle extended his hand, palm up, and Leigh placed the carrot in the center. Penny Lover's ears pricked forward and she took a step toward Kyle. He jerked his hand back. Joe, leaning against the fence, sighed, and Leigh could have kicked him.

"Keep your hand steady," Leigh instructed. "Carrots are like candy to her. Give her a piece of carrot and she'll love you forever."

Eyes wide, Kyle extended his hand again. Penny Lover walked forward, her nostrils flared.

"She looks scary," Kyle said. But he didn't move his hand.

Leigh's voice became almost a croon. "She won't hurt you. Easy. Easy. That's it."

The Appaloosa stretched her lips over the carrot and picked it up.

Kyle giggled and snatched his hand away. "She *tickled* me." Then he gazed with pride as Penny Lover crunched the carrot between her teeth. "Is that good, Penny Lover?" The horse tossed her head, and Kyle giggled again. "Can you tell if she'll have her baby today?" he asked.

Leigh had been evaluating Penny Lover the entire time she'd been inside the pen. "I doubt if it will be today," she said.

"Aw," Kyle said, his face cloudy with disappointment.

"Since she won't have her baby today, how about a picnic?" Leigh suggested as she let herself out of the corral and latched it behind her.

Kyle called a last goodbye to Penny Lover and climbed carefully down from his perch. "Where?"

"There's a beautiful little canyon with a pond not far from here. We could all go if you want."

Kyle looked at Joe. "Do you want to?"

To his credit, Joe tried to appear nonchalant. "Sure."

"How will we get there?"

He was a smart little kid, Leigh thought. "We'll take a trail ride."

Kyle shook his head. "I don't think so."

"You could ride the horse I had yesterday," Joe said. "Mikey's very gentle. You'd like him."

Kyle shook his head again.

"What if you rode Mikey with me?" Joe asked. "I could make sure you don't fall."

Kyle stood for a long moment, considering. "I'd ride with Leigh," he said at last.

Leigh's heart wrenched at the sadness that flashed in Joe's eyes before he covered it with his usual calm expression. "Okay," he said.

Leigh crouched next to Kyle. "Your dad's a terrific rider," she said. "Why don't you—"

"I said it was okay," Joe interrupted. "Now let's get going."

HIS SON WAS on a horse. Joe tried to take comfort in that as he followed Leigh and Kyle up the narrow trail into Rogue Canyon. The trouble was, Leigh was responsible for all the progress with Kyle. She had the pregnant mare that had lured Kyle to the corrals and she'd been the one to coax Kyle to climb the fence and feed carrots to Penny Lover. Now Kyle was riding a horse because he trusted Leigh to keep him from falling off. Joe was glad for all of it if that meant Kyle would begin to love the ranch, but as Leigh skillfully handled each situation with Kyle, Joe's feelings of inadequacy deepened. If there was one emotion Joe hated more than any other, it was that one.

Both fishing poles were stashed in his saddlebags. With his luck, Leigh would be a better fisherman than he was too. It was a petty thought and he brushed it aside, irritated with himself. He was probably looking for a reason to be upset with Leigh so he could distance himself from her. After their encounter on the porch, he'd tossed and turned all night. It was against his personal policy to become entangled in a relationship as complicated as this one threatened to be.

Along the trail he watched Leigh carefully as she pointed out the scarred acres blackened by the brushfire a month earlier. She seemed genuinely distressed by the destruction, but he wasn't letting her off the hook yet. He'd keep watching her, along with Freddy, Belinda and Duane. Somebody would get careless eventually.

The horses picked their way up into the canyon, their hooves clipping the rocks embedded in the trail. Joe took off his hat and wiped his forehead with his sleeve. The humidity from yesterday's rain turned the canyon into a giant sauna, but Joe didn't mind the heat. Better canyon walls than New York skyscrapers, better a hawk circling in the breeze than a flock of pigeons. Despite all his emotional turmoil since he'd arrived, he didn't regret a penny of his investment.

At last a bouquet of green farther up the canyon announced the location of the pond. When they rounded another bend, Joe could make out the rock-and-earth dam that sat astride the dry creek bed. Leigh urged Pussywillow up a steep bank to the right of the dam and he followed on Mikey, who smelled the water and nickered.

"Look, Dad!" Kyle pointed with excitement to the pond cradled by the dam. Its surface caught the reflection of cobalt sky and a crowd of majestic cottonwoods rimming the oasis. An orange dragonfly skimmed the water and barely escaped the fish leaping after it.

"Looks great, Kyle." Joe noted the size of the fish and immediately picked out two spots for casting—the sandy beach on the left side of the pond and a large rock on the back side. From either spot he should be able to avoid the reeds that swayed on the pond's far right bank.

Nudging Mikey, he rode up beside Leigh and dismounted, dropping the reins to the ground. "I'll take Kyle," he said, ducking under Mikey's neck and reaching for his son. Kyle came into his arms without hesitation, and his heart jerked with pleasure. "How'd you like the ride, buddy?" he asked as he set him on the ground.

"It was awesome!"

Joe flashed a smile at Leigh. It didn't really matter that she'd been the one to bring Kyle up here. They'd made it, and Kyle would be more than ready to go again. He returned to Mikey and opened the saddlebag. "Hey, Kyle, ready to do some fishing?"

"Okay."

Joe's happiness quotient increased. A day fishing with his son. Everything was going to be fine, just fine.

Leigh dismounted and opened her saddlebag. "I'll set up the picnic under that cottonwood tree, and we can eat whenever you want to."

Joe suddenly realized he'd only brought two poles. How stupid. "Do you want to fish? You can have one pole and Kyle can have the other. I really don't need to—"

"Don't be silly. You two go do your thing. I'll sit over here and be lazy. I brought a book, anyway."

He wondered if it was the same one he'd found in the glove compartment of her truck. "If you're sure."

"I'm sure." She gave him that mysterious, mind-bending smile of hers, the one that knocked him right on his rear. With that smile alone, she made him want her.

"Okay. Come on, Kyle. You're going to love this." As he assembled the poles and threaded the line, he wondered why he hadn't thought earlier of fishing as an activity to share with Kyle. There was nothing scary about fishing. Just a lot of thinking time, talking time. He attached a lure for Kyle and helped him cast the line out into the water.

"Now what?" Kyle asked.

"I'll cast mine out, and we'll sit and wait for the fish to come."

"Oh." Kyle stood patiently holding his pole while Joe got his line in the water. When Joe sat, Kyle sat, in exact imitation.

"Did you see how that horse Penny Lover took my carrot?" Kyle asked.

"I sure did."

"Horse lips feel funny." Kyle sat there staring at the water for a while. "I wonder what cow lips feel like. Or elephant lips."

"Or bird lips."

Kyle glanced at him, then saw he was teasing and laughed. "*Bird lips.* What about . . ." His rolled his eyes and pursed his mouth. "What about *bug* lips?"

"Don't you think ladybugs have lips?"

"No!" Kyle laughed again. Still smiling, he gazed across the pond. "I like this, Dad."

"Good. Me, too." Joe glanced over at Leigh, propped against the tree reading her book. She'd taken off her hat and sunlight filtered down through the leaves to dapple her golden hair. Joe's heart swelled with gratitude, and something else that was linked to desire, but wasn't quite the same. Something he hadn't felt in a very long time.

"She's a nice lady," Kyle said.

Joe brought his attention back to Kyle, who had noticed the direction of his glance. "Yes, she is."

"I think—"

But Joe never learned what Kyle thought. Kyle screeched as his fishing rod was nearly jerked from his hands.

"You've got a fish! Hold tight! Leigh, come hold my rod!" Joe didn't understand her peal of laughter until much later. He was too busy issuing instructions to Kyle to notice sexual innuendos.

"It's pulling really hard, Dad!" Kyle had staggered to his feet and was struggling to hold on.

Leigh arrived and Joe handed her his fishing pole. Then he crouched behind Kyle and wrapped his hands around Kyle's. "We'll pull him in gradually. Let me help you turn the reel. That's it." Joe's voice quivered with excitement. His son's first catch, and he was there. Maybe they should have the fish mounted.

"He's jumping around, Dad. Here he comes! Here he comes!"

Joe reached for the line and hauled in the bass, a respectable size for a first catch. He held it suspended by the gills as its tail flipped wildly back and forth. "A beauty, Kyle. You did great." He bestowed a proud smile on his son. Then he blinked. Kyle's face was white, his eyes wide with horror. "What's wrong, buddy? This is a great fish!"

"The hook's through his mouth, Dad! And he can't breathe. He's dying!"

"Kyle, it's a fish. We catch fish. We eat fish."

"Not me!"

"Where do you think fish sticks come from? Or those tuna sandwiches you like?"

"They don't look like that!"

"Once they did."

Kyle's lower lip quivered. "Put him back, Dad. Please. Take the hook out and put him back, so he can breathe."

Although Joe had his back to Leigh, he could feel her eyes on him. Hell, he could hear that soft, compelling voice of hers inside his head telling him to release the fish. She should stand by him on this. She lived on a ranch, for God's sake. Where did Kyle think hamburgers came from?

A tear dribbled down Kyle's cheek, making a track in the dust he'd picked up on the trail. "Please, Daddy."

Joe blew out a long, exasperated breath. The hook was imbedded pretty deep. As he tried to work it free, the bass jerked and he jabbed his thumb. Cursing under his breath he kept working, his blood mingling with that of the fish. Finally, the hook was out, and he tossed the fish back into the pond with a loud splash. It flipped its tail and disappeared beneath the surface. Kyle let out a gigantic sigh and plopped to the sand as if his legs wouldn't hold him another minute.

"I guess that's it for fishing," Joe said as he turned to Leigh. "I might as well reel that line in, too."

She handed him the fishing pole with a sympathetic glance.

"I'm leaving the issue of cows up to you," he said in an undertone.

She shrugged and gave him a small smile.

"Don't tell me you're a vegetarian."

"Pretty much."

"Swell. What's for lunch, cucumber sandwiches?"

"Roast beef for you, cheese for me and peanut butter and jelly for Kyle." She walked over to where Kyle sat on the sand and stared at the water. "The fish will be okay, Kyle."

"I sure hope so."

"Come on and help me get the sandwiches out." Leigh glanced up at the sky. "The clouds are moving in, so we'd better eat and mount up."

Joe looked up at the thunderheads forming against the mountains at the end of the canyon. After yesterday, he accorded them a lot of respect. He reeled in the line quickly and hurried to where Leigh had lunch laid out. "You're right," he said to her, tipping his head toward the clouds. "We'd better eat and run."

"I think we can stay ahead of it."

"Good. One encounter with lightning is enough for me."

She caught his eye for a moment and then quickly looked away again. "I understand."

He knew from her expression she'd read more into what he'd said than he'd intended. "I'm a simple man, Leigh. Don't look for hidden meanings."

Kyle gazed at his father. He hadn't spoken directly to him since they'd let the fish go. "What are you talking about, Dad?"

Joe couldn't imagine how he could give Kyle an explanation that would make any sense to a seven-year-old, so he didn't try. "Nothing, Kyle."

"Oh." Kyle returned his attention to his sandwich.

"Your dad thought I misunderstood him, but I don't think I did," Leigh said. "Now finish your sandwich quickly so we can get going. He's right. We don't want to get caught in the storm."

Moments later, as Joe was stashing the poles in the saddlebag, he thought he saw something move beyond the trees. A deer? He peered through the foliage, but whatever it was seemed to be gone. He turned to Leigh, who was mounting up. "Do you have deer up in this canyon?"

"A few. Why?"

"I may have just seen one."

"A deer?" Kyle gazed around. "Where?"

"It would be unusual to see a deer this time of day," Leigh said. "They prefer early morning or twilight."

"I must have been mistaken," Joe said. "Come on, buddy, and I'll lift you up in front of Leigh." He decided against suggesting Kyle ride down with him. No matter what he tried to do with the boy, it never worked out right. Apparently, he wasn't cut out to be a father to a boy like Kyle.

# 8

THE DARK CLOUDS advanced, but not fast enough to explain Leigh's uneasiness. She tried to identify the source of her worry. Maybe it was the bad business about the fish. She'd known in her heart that Kyle wouldn't like the final outcome of fishing, but she'd pushed the knowledge aside and hoped she was wrong. Joe so desperately wanted something to share with his son.

Pussywillow seemed to share Leigh's nervousness, but it could be a residual reaction to the fire. When Amanda and the baby had been trapped up in this canyon during the brushfire last month, Amanda had been riding Pussywillow. Leigh thought the gray mare had been cured of her fear of the canyon, but maybe not. Pussywillow balked on the trail several times and tossed her head.

"Leigh, what's the matter with her?" Kyle asked. He was wedged in front of her on a saddle Leigh had chosen for its roomy seat.

"Oh, she just gets twitchy sometimes." Behind them, thunder bounced across the mountain peaks, but the trail was still in sunshine.

At a switchback, Leigh glanced up at Joe following behind on Mikey. Joe had a tense set to his shoulders and a frown cut a groove between his eyebrows. The thunder rolled again, and he leaned back to study the clouds.

Leigh fought a sense of urgency. A good rider didn't push a horse down a steep trail. There was plenty of time to make it back to the ranch before the storm hit, so she had nothing to worry about. But her instincts told her she did. She scanned the empty trail ahead of her for some sign that there was a problem but could find nothing unusual. A cactus wren scolded them from the top of a saguaro, and a chipmunk skittered away from the approaching horses and riders.

"I hope Dexter wants to play Junior Scrabble today," Kyle said.

"I'm sure he's counting on it," Leigh replied. "That game really helps him remember words."

"It's fun talking to Dexter. Sometimes I pretend he's an alien trying to learn our language."

Leigh smiled. "He does have to learn a lot of things over again. They're all locked in his head, and he can't get them out."

"*I'm* going to help him get them out."

"Yes, I believe you are." Somewhere above them in the mountains, lightning hit a tree with a loud crack, and Pussywillow threw up her head. "Pat Pussywillow's neck," Leigh told Kyle. "Tell her everything's okay."

"It's okay, Pussywillow," Kyle crooned. "We're right here."

Leigh watched him and felt a moment of unexplainable terror. Kyle was so small. A lump formed in her throat and she glanced back at Joe. She wished he were following a little closer. She drew in Pussywillow's reins. "Come on, Joe," she called. "You're lagging back there."

He looked over his shoulder at the storm, then turned toward Leigh. "Mikey's doing his best. You know, I don't know what it is, but I have this funny feeling that—"

*Boom!*

The explosion shook the ground and careened off the granite walls. Kyle screamed, and Leigh fought with

Pussywillow to keep her head down as the terrified mare tried to rear.

"Leigh!" Joe shouted. Rocks clattered off the edge of the trail as he propelled Mikey toward them.

"We're okay!" she shouted back, all her attention on her plunging horse. "Don't run into us!" She brought the mare to a shivering standstill just as Joe skidded next to them. She wrapped an arm around Kyle, who had a death grip on the saddle horn and was whimpering softly.

"What the hell was that?" Joe asked, staring up the canyon in the direction of the explosion.

"Shh! Listen!" Leigh said. A soft roar grew steadily louder. When she realized what it had to be, her stomach pitched and she glanced wildly around them. They had to get up the side of the canyon. In less than a minute, a wall of water would reach them, sweeping away everything in its path.

She looked at Joe. "The dam just broke."

Panic was allowed only a temporary place in his eyes before it was replaced with fierce resolution. "We'll make it out."

"You take Kyle with you. Mikey's a stronger horse, and he's better in chaotic situations."

Joe's jaw flexed. "Then you and Kyle get on him and I'll take Pussywillow."

"No." The roaring grew louder, accompanied by ripping noises as undergrowth was torn from the canyon floor. "We don't have time to argue. I'm a better rider."

"All the more reason for you to take him on Mikey! We're not going to argue, because I'm telling you—"

"I wanna stay with Leigh!" Kyle wailed.

"See?"

"Just do it, Joe. I don't think I have the strength to hold him while we go up." Birds flew down the canyon, animals sought higher ground as the earth trembled.

His expression was grim. "All right. Come here, Kyle."

"No!"

"Now, Kyle!"

Leigh leaned close to the trembling boy. "This is an order from your captain, Mr. Spock," she murmured, holding him tight, trying to convey strength. "The success of the mission depends on it. I'm counting on you. And you'll have to be very quiet, so you don't scare Mikey."

After a tense moment, he nodded.

She lifted him from the saddle and into Joe's arms. She had to shout to be heard above the deafening sound of the water that was nearly upon them. "Get Mikey up the side of that hill! I'll be right behind you!" She hoped. Mikey was steady and well-trained enough to go up the hill. She wasn't so sure about Pussywillow.

Joe clamped an arm around Kyle, pointed Mikey at the hill and dug in his heels. The horse plunged upward, scrabbling to gain its footing on the loose rock. Leigh held her breath and silently urged them on. She'd made the right decision. She didn't have Joe's upper-body strength and she would never have been able to keep her seat and hold on to Kyle at the same time.

Snorting and heaving, Mikey gained a yard, two yards, slid back a foot, gained another two. Joe's shoulder muscles bunched as he kept a tight hold on Kyle with one arm and grasped the reins in the other hand.

After what seemed like hours, enough room opened up behind them and Leigh pointed Pussywillow in the same direction. The mare wouldn't budge. Leigh stroked and patted, crooned and demanded. The sound of rushing water grew close, very close.

"I should leave you here, you bag of bones," Leigh muttered. "But I won't. We'll try this another way." She dismounted and started up the hill, the reins in her hand. They tightened as Pussywillow continued to balk. "Come on, girl," Leigh called. She clucked and whistled, promised treats and apologized for calling the mare a bag of bones. Then the roar became deafening, and she looked up the canyon and saw the water.

Suddenly, all she could think of was the old movie clip of Moses parting the Red Sea. The water advanced down the narrow canyon, a ten-foot-high blade scraping everything clean as it passed. Nothing could survive being carried along in the torrent.

"Come on!" Leigh shouted, yanking on the reins.

Pussywillow took a step forward, then another.

"That's it!" Leigh climbed higher, pulled harder. Pussywillow followed, but she was going too slow. "You stupid horse," Leigh cried, pulling until she thought her arm would come out of its socket.

Then a strong hand wrenched the reins from her. Joe was beside her, hauling the horse up the slope, yelling at her to go on up to Kyle.

She glanced at the wall of water bearing down on them and shook her head.

Joe's eyes blazed. His shout was nearly obliterated by the oncoming water as he tugged on the terrorized horse's reins. "Go! He needs you more than he needs me!"

"That's not true, you bullheaded dope! There's no dealing with you, is there?"

Joe stared at her. Then his mustache twitched as the corner of his mouth lifted in a half smile and he shook his head. "Go," he murmured. For good measure, he gave her a swift whack on the behind.

Recognizing the stubborn Scorpio will in action, she started up the slope. Kyle couldn't be left alone, and Joe would wrestle with that horse until the water arrived. She knew that more surely than anything else in the world. Grasping at bushes and outcroppings, she climbed toward the ridge where he'd left Kyle and Mikey. She could see a portion of the bay horse, but no sign of Kyle. He must be petrified.

"We're coming, Kyle!" she called, not knowing if he'd be able to hear her over the crash of the torrent below or if the term *we* was accurate.

When she was nearly to the ledge, she looked back. Joe had made some progress, but not enough. The water surged just below him, gradually slicing the ground from beneath Pussywillow's hind feet.

"Joe! Leave her!" she screamed.

He dropped the reins, but instead of abandoning the mare, he lunged for the bridle and yanked. For once, Pussywillow acted in her own interests and leapt forward just as the last bit of support slid from behind her. Horse and man scrambled, slid back, scrambled some more.

And made it.

Leigh sat down where she was, covered her eyes and began to weep. Slowly she became aware of a small arm around her shoulders, and a hand patting her arm.

"Don't cry," Kyle said, sounding as if he would burst into tears himself at any moment. "Don't cry, Leigh."

She sniffed and wiped at her eyes just as Joe reached the spot where she sat.

He adjusted his grip on Pussywillow's bridle and gazed down at her without speaking. Finally, he cleared his throat. "Why aren't you two up on the ledge with Mikey?"

Kyle looked up at his father. "I came to be with Leigh."

An immense sadness filled his eyes and he looked away. "Yeah, I can see that, buddy. I can see that plain as day."

THE DANGER WAS OVER so quickly it seemed incredible to Joe that it had ever existed. In a matter of minutes the water level began to recede, until finally only the creek bed ran full. But a shadow passed over the sun, and Joe remembered that they still had an impending thunderstorm to worry about.

"Let's go." He started the laborious process of turning Pussywillow around.

"The trail will be wiped out," Leigh said. "Want me to lead?"

"I can handle it. You bring Kyle on Mikey." He made himself say it, feeling the pain of knowing that Leigh was a better choice for taking care of his son than he was. If she hadn't told him to, Kyle wouldn't have ridden with him up the hill. Kyle depended more on a woman he'd known three days than on Joe, his own father. Sometimes Joe found it difficult to believe Kyle was really his son, although he didn't doubt the biological fact of it. But there seemed to be nothing of Joe's spirit in this boy, nothing to connect them except for a last name. And Emerson Pope would love to change even that. Maybe Joe was wrong to fight it.

The trip back was tough as they worked their way around uprooted trees, their roots reaching into the sky like sea anemones, and boulders the size of sedans wedged against piles of debris. Any minute, Joe expected the thunderstorm to strike, but instead the clouds edged north along the mountains, moving gradually out of range, grumbling as they departed.

When the bedraggled group was nearly out of the canyon, Joe heard a shout and answered it. From around a dislodged boulder Ry and Freddy came riding toward them, their faces taut with strain.

"Thank God!" Freddy cried, urging her horse forward. "We heard the explosion and rode out to investigate. When we saw the water in Rogue Creek, and no sign of you . . ." She swallowed. "Where were you when the dam gave way?"

"On the trail coming back," Joe said, his gaze swinging toward Ry, who looked grim as death.

Freddy gasped.

"Hey, sis," Leigh said, coming up beside Joe. "Am I glad to see you."

Freddy's eyes brimmed. "I'm pretty thrilled about it, myself. Come on, let's get you all home again so I can have a nervous breakdown."

Joe glanced at Ry. "It doesn't look as if we'll have that storm this afternoon, so if you have the time, I'd like you to come back up the canyon with me," he said.

"Sure thing. Freddy can go back with Leigh and Kyle." Ry sounded casual, but Joe knew by the set of his jaw that he was anything but relaxed.

Freddy looked from her husband's stern expression to Joe's determined one and nodded. "Let me switch mounts with you, Joe. Pussywillow looks done in. You'll do much better on Maureen."

Joe rubbed the gray mare's neck. "I'm sure Pussywillow would appreciate that. She's had a bad day." He swung down from the saddle.

Kyle turned wide blue eyes on him. He hadn't spoken since they'd climbed down the hill and started home. "Will the water come back again, Dad?"

Joe paused. "No, Kyle. That was all the water from the pond, and it's drained now."

Kyle drew in a sharp breath. "The fish! What about the fish?"

Joe heaved a sigh. He didn't believe in holding out false hopes to anyone. It only prolonged the agony. "I don't think they made it, buddy. I'm sorry."

"Daddy!" Kyle's cry was almost an accusation. "Can't you save them when you go back up there?"

"I don't think we can, son."

"Your father saved *us*, Kyle," Leigh said. "And didn't you see the way he pulled Pussywillow up the hill? If he hadn't done that, she would have been swept away too."

Joe knew she was only trying to help, but it was humiliating that she even had to try. He sought her gaze. "I'd appreciate it if you'd just get him home for me," he said softly.

"I will." Her eyes were deep with unspoken sympathy.

"Thanks." He turned away. Taking the reins that Freddy handed him, he swung up on Maureen and followed Ry up the canyon.

Viewing the damage after the adrenaline rush was gone made his stomach turn, especially when he thought of what could have happened to Kyle and Leigh. In the Bronx he'd seen the rubble left when a tenement house had been bombed as part of gang retaliation. This was a little like that, except the bodies were of animals caught in the destruction instead of people. Joe could easily imagine people instead. Specific people. That was the difference between a cop's imagination and a civilian's, he thought. A civilian might be afraid of death, but in general terms. A cop had seen enough to make those terms very specific.

"What do you think we'll find when we get up there?" Ry asked over his shoulder.

"I hope we'll find evidence of dynamite. Maybe some footprints, hoofprints of a horse. I saw something when we were up there for our picnic, something I thought was a deer. I think it was our guy."

"Unfortunately, you're not going to be able to prove much from footprints or hoofprints. The True Love has traditionally given hikers and trail riders access into the mountains through Rogue Canyon. Matter of fact, I think Duane brought a breakfast ride up this morning. The pond's a popular spot. At least it was a popular spot."

"Then Duane could have planted a timed explosive?"

Ry didn't reply right away. "I guess he could have."

"Whoever did this is a reckless bastard," Joe said. "Maybe he'll also start getting careless."

"I hope this incident convinces you it couldn't have been Freddy or Leigh."

Joe had been giving that some thought. He didn't answer right away.

Ry swiveled in his saddle. "Joe? Come on, man. Leigh could have been killed today, along with you and Kyle. You saw how Freddy reacted, too. And you just suggested the person is a man."

"I don't think either of them executed this, if that's what you mean. But suppose they started something they don't know how to stop? Suppose they hired somebody in the beginning, and that person has decided to take command of the operation?"

Ry shook his head. "Freddy couldn't keep something like that from me this long. I'd sense it, or she'd break down. If I thought she was capable of hiding a secret that horrible, I'd have to question the validity of our whole relationship."

Joe gazed up the canyon. Was it the aftermath of battle, or only the beginning of the fight? "I hope that won't become necessary," he said.

"It won't."

"And maybe Freddy doesn't know anything. Maybe it's Leigh who started the ball rolling." The words sat bitterly on his tongue, but he had to say them.

"You're wrong, Joe. Leigh has a reverence for life. Even if your original supposition was true, and Leigh had hired someone to make mischief around the True Love, she'd have exposed that person after the brushfire, no matter what the consequences to her." Ry swept his arm to encompass the battered canyon. "She'd have gone to jail before she would have allowed something like this to happen."

Joe wanted to believe him, but Ry wasn't a reliable source. He'd fallen in love with the ranch and its foreman. "Well, this joker has my full attention, now," Joe said. "I'm on this case full-time. I'm even considering sending Kyle back to his mother, since I can't spend time with him."

"I would hate to see you do that," Ry said. "I know how much it meant to you, bringing him out. Maybe you'll wrap this up quickly. Belinda and Dexter can keep an eye on him, and Leigh seems to have taken a real shine to him."

"Yeah. A real shine." Joe hesitated. "The thing is, even if I could spend time with Kyle, he probably wouldn't want me to."

"Hey, I doubt that."

"We just don't operate on the same wavelength, Ry. I've tried, but we keep missing the connection. I'm making us both miserable."

Ry didn't respond right away, and the silence was filled with the crunch of the horses' hooves in the streambed. Finally, he said, "This is going to sound corny as hell, but I'll say it, anyway. The True Love has a way of helping you sort out stuff like this."

"Now you sound like Leigh."

"I know it. A few months ago I would have choked before admitting that a place could have . . . well, like a *healing* effect on people. Living with asphalt and concrete all my life, I couldn't imagine what a ride through the desert on a good horse could do for me."

Joe laughed. "The way I heard it, you ended up so saddle sore you could barely stand up."

"That, too." Ry guided his horse carefully over a fallen tree. "Who knows, maybe it won't happen for you. I was just a paperpusher back in New York, but out here . . ."

"I know what you mean. It's the way the dust smells, the way the shadows change on the mountains."

"The sunsets."

"The thunderstorms," Joe said. He'd loved that storm yesterday, he realized now. It wasn't very rational to tempt lightning that way, but he hadn't been operating rationally, especially after Leigh arrived.

"It's up to you, of course, but I wouldn't send Kyle back just yet," Ry said. "Give it some time. I don't think you'll regret it."

"Hell, I have so many regrets now, a few more wouldn't matter, anyway."

# 9

LEIGH UNDERSTOOD that Joe had to make the investigation top priority. He and Ry had found evidence of dynamite at the ruined dam, and the whole future of the ranch was at stake. Yet, she thought Joe was carrying his absorption in the case too far. For the past three days, he'd spent virtually no time with Kyle. True, he spent his days and some of his nights talking to anyone who might have information he could use, and he had reason to be tired and distracted. But Leigh suspected Joe was using the admittedly legitimate excuse of the investigation to avoid painful contact with a son he didn't understand.

Kyle made do, Leigh noticed. He played Junior Scrabble with Dexter a lot and swam in the pool under Belinda's watchful eye. Leigh set up the adobe block project, and she and Dexter spent an afternoon out behind the patio wall teaching Kyle how to make the sun-dried bricks. They'd had to erect a plastic tent to keep the adobe dry during the afternoon rain, but the blocks had turned out fine. Kyle had used them to build a shelter for his Star Trek action figures.

To someone who didn't look closely, Kyle might have seemed perfectly happy, but Leigh watched Kyle with the empathy of a kindred spirit. She noticed each time he looked longingly after his departing father, and the slump to his shoulders after Joe had dismissed an overture for attention by saying he had to discuss something with Ry.

Apparently, Joe had decided to ignore Leigh, too. His words to her were few, and if from time to time he glanced her way, he turned his head the minute she tried to meet his gaze. After two earth-shattering kisses, he'd closed himself off. Textbook Scorpio—stubborn and wary. But knowing that didn't ease the ache in her heart.

Still, she thought she and Kyle were coping well under the circumstances and she'd decided not to make an issue of Joe's behavior. Until today, however, when she looked out the living room window and saw Kyle fishing in the swimming pool with a fishing pole made from a stick, a string and a rock tied to the end of it. Chloe, Dexter's dog, lay beside Kyle, her head on her paws. The sight of that lonely little boy sitting cross-legged by the pool pretending to fish broke her heart.

She walked through the French doors onto the patio and Kyle looked up, his Spock ears still resting on the underside of his cowboy hat. Leigh smiled whenever she saw those ears. Joe didn't realize it, but Kyle's stubborn insistence on wearing the ears was evidence enough he was Joe's son.

"Hi, Leigh," Kyle said. Chloe lifted her head and smacked her shaggy tail on the concrete.

"Hi, yourself." She took a deep breath of the rain-scented air. A storm had passed through a few minutes earlier, washing away the intense heat. Scattered clouds remained, blocking out the punishing afternoon sun. "It's nice out here. Mind if I join you and Chloe?"

"No, but I only got one fishing pole."

"That's okay." Leigh grabbed a plastic chair cushion and set it down next to Kyle on the damp concrete. "Isn't your behind getting wet?"

"Yeah." Kyle grinned. "I don't care. Chloe doesn't care, either."

"I guess you're both tougher than I am, then." Leigh lowered herself to the cushion and sat quietly, waiting to see if Kyle would talk.

"This is the part of fishing I like," he said at last. "You can just sit and think. Or if somebody's with you, you can talk a little bit. I've been talking to Chloe."

Leigh's heart squeezed. "That is a good part of fishing."

"I don't like the catching fish part."

"Me, neither."

Kyle sighed, and it was much too grown-up a sound to have come from a seven-year-old.

Leigh waited, letting him choose his moment, his way of communicating his problem.

"Like I've been telling Chloe, my dad sure is busy," Kyle said at last.

"It takes a lot of time, trying to find out who blew up that dam."

"Don't worry. Dad will catch them. He's the best."

Leigh gazed into the turquoise water of the pool. "I'm sure he is."

Kyle raised his pole a little and the stone tied to the end bobbed to a different spot on the bottom of the pool. He sighed again. "The trouble is, my dad hates me."

Leigh gasped and turned to him. "Oh, no, Kyle! He loves you more than anything!" That much she knew. Joe couldn't express his love, but she never thought for a moment it didn't exist.

But Kyle shook his head. "He thinks I'm a wimp because I like Star Trek stuff, and I'm scared to ride a horse by myself, and I don't like catching fish. I bet he wishes he had a different boy."

Leigh wrapped her arm around his shoulders. "More likely he wishes he could be a different kind of dad."

"Different?" Kyle looked at her in surprise. "But he's perfect the way he is!"

A lump lodged in her throat. "So are you," she murmured.

"No, I'm not. I get scared. I get scared a lot."

She gazed into his blue eyes and debated how much to say. "Everybody gets scared sometimes."

Kyle returned his attention to his fishing pole. "Not my dad."

"Even your dad." Instinct made her glance toward the living room window. Somehow, she'd known Joe would be there, watching them. She caught the bleak yearning in his expression before he realized he'd been discovered and walked away from the window.

Apparently, Kyle had been too wrapped up in his misery to notice the figure at the window. "My dad's not afraid of anything," he maintained, his chin jutting out.

He looked so much like Joe at that moment that Leigh had a sudden insight. What if Joe had been a sensitive little kid, just like Kyle? Maybe he'd been teased, hurt, disgraced somehow. Someone with a protective instinct as developed as Joe's would want to make sure his son didn't suffer the same fate. The only way to do that was to toughen the kid up and help him build a shell around himself just like his father had.

"Kyle, I'm going to tell you something about me, something I don't talk about with people unless I trust them. Can I trust you?"

Kyle turned to her and nodded so hard his hat flipped off. He grabbed it and put it back on, careful not to crush the Spock ears.

"All my life I've been able to . . . sense things. I'm sort of like a radio that picks up waves. If I tune in, I can sometimes tell what people are thinking. If I really concentrate, I can tell what animals are thinking."

"Cool! What's Chloe thinking?"

Leigh hesitated, then focused on the dog. She smiled. "She's thinking that damp concrete feels good. And that she likes the way you smell."

Kyle laughed and scratched behind the dog's ears. "I like the way she smells, too. We can't have a dog in my mom and stepdad's apartment, but I sure would like to have Chloe live with me. Would you like that, Chloe?"

Chloe licked his hand.

"I don't think she would," Kyle said, looking back at Leigh. "No rabbits to chase, no horses, no Dexter."

"You see? You can figure out what animals are thinking, too."

Kyle looked startled. Then he shook his head. "I was just guessing."

"I think with practice you could do more than guess."

"Wow. That would be cool."

Leigh smiled down at him. She could really grow to love this kid. "I had a specific reason for telling you about this ability I have. First of all, do you believe me?"

Kyle nodded.

"Then listen very carefully. Your dad doesn't hate you. He loves you very much. He'd like for you and he to be better friends, but he hasn't figured out yet how to make that happen."

Doubt struggled with hope in Kyle's blue eyes. "You saw that in his mind?"

"Absolutely."

Hope won, and a tiny smile played at the corners of his mouth.

"So think about that while you and Chloe are fishing, okay?"

"Okay."

"I have a few things to take care of, but I'll see you at dinner." Leigh pushed herself upright and picked up the chair cushion.

"Yep," Kyle said happily, his face lit with joy. "See you at dinner."

LEIGH HURRIED toward the French doors. With luck Joe was somewhere nearby, and he was going to listen to what she had to say if she had to rope him and tie him to a post to keep him in one spot.

Joe was no longer in the living room, but Rosa, the head housekeeper, was there supervising a new girl who was cleaning the cobwebs from the high, beamed ceiling.

"Did either of you see where Mr. Gilardini went?" Leigh asked.

Rosa propped her hands on her hips. "Out on the porch, I think. *Sí*. The porch."

But Joe wasn't there anymore, either. Leigh gazed around in frustration. Then she started down the flagstone walk. She'd told Kyle she could read minds, and many times she could. Right now, she had to connect with Joe's if she expected to locate him. The ranch was a big place.

At the end of the walk she paused and glanced at the sandy ground. There were boot prints in the moist earth and the prints led off to the left. She followed them, knowing that she could be tracking anybody in a pair of cowboy boots. But intuition told her she was following Joe. A path beyond the parking area led to a seldom-used picnic spot in a grove of mesquite trees. Leigh had vague memories of family picnics there when she was very young and her mother was still alive. But with one rickety picnic table and no fireplace for cooking, it wasn't a practical spot for feeding ranch guests, and few people knew it was even there.

The tang of wet creosote bushes spiced the air. The green bark of a nearby palo verde tree gleamed as if it had been shellacked, and in its branches hung a cobweb woven with diamonds. Bring water to the desert and amazing things happened, Leigh thought. Flowers bloomed where only thorns had been before. If only such a transformation could be wrought in people. Perhaps what some people needed was a cleansing storm.

Her boots crunched along the sandy path as she walked toward the picnic area. She made no attempt to approach quietly. She was through pussyfooting around Joe Gilardini.

He sat on the table, his feet propped on the attached bench. His expression was guarded as he watched her come toward him. "There must be some Indian blood in your ancestry," he said. "Tracking me all the way out here."

She stopped and braced herself for the fray. "Maybe I should just stake you over an anthill and pour honey on you, come to think of it."

Joe nudged his hat back with his thumb. "And to what do I owe this flood of hostility?"

She threw her anger at him as if hurling a bolt of lightning. "Your general stupidity."

"That comes as no surprise. I never claimed to be a genius."

She aimed again, determined to crack his armor. "How about a father? Did you ever claim to be that?"

His eyes darkened and he stepped down from the table. "I should have known this would be about Kyle. I saw you out there having a little talk with him while he fished with that stick of his."

"Don't you dare make fun of that fishing pole."

He came closer. "If I don't, some other kid will. The way I look at it, it's my job to—"

"Make him tough?"

"Somebody has to."

"And make him think you hate him?"

He recoiled as if she'd slapped him. His mask slipped. "What?"

"That's what he thinks. And considering all your macho instructions, your disapproval, your long absences lately, it's no wonder. He has every reason to suppose that—"

Joe grabbed her by the shoulders, his eyes reflecting the storm in hers. "How could he think I hate him? Did you plant that in his head? Because if you did, so help me, I'll—"

"*You* planted it in his head, you idiot! You've given him the idea that there's something wrong with him because he's not as fearless as you are. He doesn't realize that *you're* the cowardly one, running away from any show of emotion, running away from anybody who might make you *feel* something." She gasped for breath, drawing the warm, wet air into her lungs, the scent of ripe earth into her nostrils. Her heart fluttered like a bird's.

A muscle worked in his jaw as he glared down at her. "You're nothing but trouble. I figured that out the first time I saw you."

"You think *you* have trouble with *me*? I wish you'd never set foot on this ranch! Of all the men in the world, it had to be you—a proud, suspicious, stubborn *Scorpio*. Fate couldn't send me a gentle Pisces or a fun-loving

Libra, or a kindhearted Aquarius. No, I have to end up with you!"

He gave her a shake. "End up with? What in hell are you talking about?"

"This." She stood trembling in his arms, drowning in the sensation of his touch. "Don't tell me you can't feel what happens whenever we get within ten feet of each other."

His grip tightened and flames danced in his eyes. "That's the dumbest thing I've ever heard. Maybe there's some basic animal attraction between us, but I'm no victim of fate. Neither are you."

"Then let go of me," she murmured, knowing he would not, could not.

"In a minute." He drew her closer, swept her hat from her head and tossed it on the table behind him.

"Why not now?" she taunted as her mouth moistened for his kiss and her body tightened and throbbed for even more.

"Because I choose not to."

She closed her eyes. "That's what you think."

His mustache tickled her upper lip as he paused. "Shut up, Leigh," he said softly.

Then he was there, and nothing mattered but this. He pulled her in, setting her heart in motion as surely as the moon swelled the tides. His tongue sought entrance and she gave it—unable to resist giving whatever he called forth in her. Exchanging breath for breath, they kissed deeper, and deeper yet, strengthening the connection made in that first glance, that first touch.

She arched against him, feeling the familiar imprint of his body. She didn't know when they would make love—perhaps not even in this existence. But they would make love. It was inevitable. She would smooth the rough, raw edges of his soul with the nectar of desire; he would slake her thirst for cataclysmic passion. Because at last she understood. She was not destined for a gentle love filled with soft sighs and dewy looks. She was born for the whirlwind.

He'd unfastened the first two buttons of her blouse before his hand stilled and his mouth lifted from hers. He was breathing hard. "There's no such thing as star-crossed lovers," he managed to say.

She greeted his statement with a soft laugh.

He moved his hand from the buttons of her blouse up the column of her throat to her chin, where he tilted it back so he could look into her eyes. "You're beautiful and I want you, simple as that. A normal man-woman thing."

She struggled for breath. "And you always have this strong a reaction to the beautiful women you meet? In a city like New York, where fashion models walk down the street every day, you must be in a perpetual state of arousal."

"No, I don't, but the pressures are different there. The pace is faster. There's not as much time to think about..." As he gazed down at her, he seemed to lose his train of thought. Naked passion flared in his eyes. "All right. I've never wanted anybody like this," he admitted. "I want to rip your clothes off and take you right here on the picnic table."

"Why don't you?"

He caught his breath. "God, you're sassy."

"Get used to it, cowboy."

"That's like asking a horse to get used to a burr under his saddle."

"I couldn't have said it better. When are you going to let loose and take that saddle off? Burrs aren't a problem if you ride bareback."

He groaned and pulled her tight against him. "I've tried so hard to stay away from you. I need a clear head for this investigation, and you turn my brains to mush."

"You're making the mistake most cops make, trying to solve a case with logic. If you'd let me help, I could save you a lot of time."

His gaze narrowed. "With your 'powers' you could lead me to the person who's doing this?"

"Maybe. I could certainly tell you who isn't doing it."

"Okay."

She was taken aback. He'd capitulated to her methods too easily. "Okay?"

"Sure. I'll use any information that comes my way. Go ahead."

She backed out of his arms. "You're stringing me along, aren't you?"

"No. I'd honestly like to hear your opinion."

She studied his expression and believed his statement, as far as it went. But something didn't feel right. "We can discuss the case later. The most important issue right now is Kyle. He's probably still sitting out by the pool, and he desperately needs some attention from you. That's what I came out here to accomplish. But somehow, when we're alone . . ." Her gaze sought his and her body responded to the banked desire in the depths of his eyes. Warmth rushed through her. On this level of communication, she had no doubts.

His hands clenched at his sides and his breathing quickened. "My God, you test a man's control." His look burned as it swept over her, as if making an unspoken promise that the fire raging between them would be dealt with soon. "Go on back. I'll follow in a minute."

Leigh did as he suggested, not because she was willing to comply with his orders, but because, at the moment, a little boy's needs were more important than her own.

When she reached the ranch house, an unfamiliar BMW sat in the parking area outside the low adobe wall. She hurried down the flagstone walk, her instincts on red alert. Opening the front door, she found Kyle and Belinda standing with a chunky man, whose silk tie looked uncomfortably tight around the collar of his white dress shirt. He wore glasses and was beginning to grow bald. But the most important thing about him was the way he rested his hand on Kyle's shoulder.

Belinda glanced at Leigh. Her expression was distraught, but she maintained her poise and spoke with her usual pleasant manner. "This is Emerson J. Pope, Kyle's stepfather," she said, confirming what Leigh had suspected. "Mr. Pope, this is Leigh Singleton, our head wrangler."

Pope turned, but he didn't offer her his hand. "Kyle called his mother yesterday," he said. "His stories of rampaging bulls and flash floods made her hysterical with worry. We're convinced this isn't a safe environment for the boy. I've come to take him home."

# 10

JOE LEANED his backside against the picnic table with a sigh. Folding his arms, he studied the damp, sandy ground at his feet. Leigh was so tuned in to him that he'd have to be very careful. She wanted to help him with the investigation. This could be her way of leading him to the person she'd hired and ending the destruction without implicating herself. Maybe she was in league with Eb Whitlock. He hated to think it, but he had to stay objective, despite the way she heated his blood. Even despite her good intentions with Kyle.

He now believed she really wanted to help him connect with his son. So, Kyle thought he hated him. Funny, Joe had figured it the other way around. He thought Kyle didn't have much use for his rough, crude father, the fish killer. Every move Joe had made seemed to be the wrong one, so he'd relegated himself to the role of bad guy, the unpopular person destined to teach Kyle about reality. But he didn't want Kyle to think he hated him. He loved the little guy, Spock ears and all. Yet he'd never said so, never felt comfortable with stating his feelings straight out like that. And gushing about love wouldn't help the kid toughen up, which he desperately needed to do if he was to survive.

Joe started up the path and thought about what he could say to Kyle that would convince the boy he didn't hate him. Maybe he could tell him how proud he'd been that Kyle had fended for himself while his dad had been busy with the investigation. That would reinforce self-reliance. Joe could admire the adobe blocks Kyle had made and compliment him on picking up a new skill, which conveyed another good message.

As he reached the ranch house, he felt better about the coming conversation with Kyle. At least he had a plan. He noticed the relatively clean BMW sitting outside the adobe wall and wondered who had driven in from town. Most of the people in the area had pickup trucks, and with all the rain that had fallen recently, the fenders were usually crusted with mud.

Striding down the walk, he went over what he would say to Kyle. He wouldn't make fun of the stick-and-string fishing pole. Leigh had been right about that. Better to keep away from the subject of fishing altogether. He opened the front door and started inside. Then suddenly, he stopped, one hand still on the door handle, and stared at Emerson J. Pope.

Pope stared back.

"What the hell are you doing here?" Joe bellowed.

"You weren't entirely candid about conditions out at this ranch, were you, Joe?" Pope said. "Hardly a place for a small boy, wouldn't you say?"

Joe's gaze shot from Pope to Leigh, who looked upset, to Belinda, who looked grief stricken, to Kyle, who looked cowed. "What do you mean, *conditions?*" he asked, turning back to Pope. "Talk like a normal human being, if that's possible."

Pope's cheek twitched, a tic that had caused him some problems in the courtroom, Joe happened to know. Joe had liked nothing better than quizzing cops who had testified at trials where Pope had been the lawyer for the defense. Especially trials where Pope lost. Unfortunately, that didn't happen often enough to suit Joe.

"I'm referring to the bull incident," Pope said. "As if that weren't bad enough, you took the child into the middle of a lethal flash flood. Darlene instructed me to bring him back to New York. I'm prepared to get a court order, if necessary."

"You son of a—" Joe remembered Kyle and censored his language. "Is that what Kyle wants?"

"I'm not prepared to let a seven-year-old make that sort of decision. He's coming with me."

"Not if he doesn't want to, he's not."

"Look, Gilardini, don't make me use the power of the courts. I—"

The front door swung open and Freddy burst into the room. "Leigh! I called from the corrals earlier but you weren't here, so I drove up—" She noticed a stranger in the room and paused.

"This is Kyle's stepfather, Emerson J. Pope," Leigh said. "Why did you want me?"

"Penny Lover's showing all the signs. Since it's her first foal, I know it could be a while, but I think you'd better get down there. Duane's with her now."

Kyle broke free of his stepfather's grip and rushed toward Freddy. "Penny Lover's going to have her baby?"

Freddy grinned. "I think so. Want to watch?"

"Boy, do I!"

Pope cleared his throat. "I have return plane reservations for both of us in three hours. That leaves just enough time for Kyle to pack and for me to return the rental car. He won't be able to go with you to the stables, or whatever you're talking about."

"No!" Kyle whirled toward his stepfather. "I have to stay, Em! Penny Lover's going to have her *baby.*"

Joe stepped closer to Pope. "He's staying."

Pope adjusted his glasses. "I'm afraid not. I promised Darlene that—"

Leigh edged her way between the two men. "I have a suggestion. Why don't you stay at the True Love tonight as our guest, Mr. Pope? I'm sure you can change your plane reservations, and Kyle's mother can't possibly be worried about him now that you're on the scene. Kyle has been waiting for this foal to be born, and I hardly think you want to deprive him of an educational experience I'm sure you couldn't duplicate in New York City. You're welcome to come down to the corrals, yourself, if you like."

Joe watched with interest as Leigh turned up her compelling gaze to full wattage. Joe knew well the effect of that wise serenity.

Pope squirmed and finally looked away. "I—ah—see your point. The boy is very bright—gifted, in fact. Darlene's family is very intelligent. She's always trying to expose Kyle to new experiences, challenge his intellectual capacity. Let me call her and discuss the situation."

"Leigh," Freddy said, urgency in her voice. "We have to go."

Leigh gave a slight nod and returned her attention to Pope. "By all means, call her. Belinda can reach us down at the corrals if your wife still insists that you and Kyle be on that plane tonight, but I have a hunch she won't." She put out her hand to Kyle. "Let's go."

Kyle took it and looked up at Joe. "Are you coming, Dad?"

"Wouldn't miss it for the world." Joe fell into step beside Kyle as Freddy led the way out the door. Behind them, Belinda directed Pope to the phone.

When they were all safely headed down the walk toward Freddy's truck, Joe glanced over at Leigh. "That was one of the slickest things I've ever seen."

Leigh just smiled, but Freddy laughed outright. "You don't want to get into a verbal contest with my sister."

"But that guy's a trial lawyer!" Joe said.

"But Leigh read his mind," Kyle said. "Didn't you, Leigh? That's how you knew what to say."

Leigh flicked a glance at Joe before smiling down at Kyle. "I could see that your stepfather really had your best interests at heart, so I simply pointed out that in this case, it would be in your best interests to stay and watch Penny Lover give birth. It's true, after all."

"It sure is!" Kyle said, almost skipping along beside her.

"Somebody's going to have to ride in the back of the truck," Freddy said. "All four of us can't squeeze into the seat."

"I'll ride in back," Joe volunteered.

"Me, too!" Kyle said.

"No, I'm afraid not," Joe said. "I don't want your stepfather taking a look outside and discovering I allowed you to ride in the back of a pickup. He has enough charges racked up against me already. I wonder how he found out about the flood and the bull?"

Kyle looked miserable, but he squared his shoulders and faced his father. "I called and told Mom. It's my fault, Dad. All this is my fault."

Joe met the admission with a swell of pride. "It took guts to tell me that, Kyle. Congratulations."

"Then you're not mad at me?"

"Of course not." He gave Kyle's hat a tug. "Now get in the truck. We have business down at the corrals."

Leigh held the door as Kyle clambered into Freddy's muddy white truck. Just before she got in, she glanced back at Joe. Her smile was bright enough to light the universe. Or at least his corner of it. He grinned back and vaulted into the truck bed. He'd never met a woman to equal Leigh Singleton.

TWO HOURS LATER, quite a festive group had gathered around Penny Lover's corral as the mare took her time about going into labor. Joe stood leaning against the fence with Ry and Duane while Duane told stories of previous births and Ry kept wondering aloud if he ought to send somebody into town for cigars. For the moment, Kyle sat on the top rail right next to Joe's shoulder. He alternated between that perch and standing between Freddy and Leigh while the two women stroked and crooned to the expectant mare.

The other hands kept dropping by the corral to check on Penny Lover's progress. Joe's three days of familiarizing himself with everything about the ranch had included learning their names. Curtis was the tall blonde; the guy with the big belly and mustache was Davis; and everyone called the earnest young kid with freckles Rusty.

They all seemed to have adopted Kyle. Curtis and Davis even coaxed Kyle over to pet Romeo in his pen behind the tack shed.

"He's pretty nice, really," Kyle confided to Joe afterward.

Ry had arrived about an hour ago, bringing with him a message from Emerson J. Pope. He and Kyle's mother had decided Kyle could remain another night and witness the birth of the foal. Pope had decided to stay at a resort closer to town, where he could get what he termed "a decent meal." Joe was determined to make the most of this reprieve.

Duane bit off a chaw of tobacco and tucked it under his lip. "Any of you city fellers ever seen anythin' born?"

"Nope," Ry said. "This will be good practice for when Freddy has a baby."

Freddy looked over her shoulder at him. "Does that mean you expect me to give birth in the middle of a corral?"

Ry nudged back his hat and winked at her. "Sure would save a pile of money, sweetheart."

The hands all laughed, and Joe grinned, shaking his head at his partner. He'd bet Ry and Freddy would be trading barbs on their fiftieth wedding anniversary.

"I've never seen anything born," Kyle said. "Have you, Dad?"

"Yep." Joe poked Kyle gently in the middle of his chest. "You."

"You *did*? I didn't know that."

"Best day of my life," Joe said.

"It was?" Kyle's eyes shone with eagerness. "What did I look like?"

"A bright red monkey."

"*Dad.*"

"A handsome bright red monkey." *And I was so happy, I cried when the doctor handed you to me*. But this wasn't the time or place to say that. Joe wasn't sure if there was a good time to admit something so personal. Even Darlene hadn't noticed, because he'd turned away before she could see the tears streaming down his face, the tears that had dripped onto that screaming, bloody, fantastic miracle of life that was his son.

Leigh left her charge for a moment and walked over to the fence where Kyle was sitting. "I'm not sure when things will get started around here," she said, her eyes encompassing both father and son. "Maybe you'd like to go back up to the house and have something to eat."

"I don't want to leave," Kyle said. "I might miss it."

"I could go and get Belinda to pack us a picnic or something," Joe offered.

"That's a thought." She stood in the glow from the setting sun, surrounded by light the color of ripe peaches. Joe had never wanted to kiss someone so much in his life.

"I tell you what we're gonna do," Duane said. He paused to spit on the ground. "Penny Lover would prob'ly appreciate it if we'd move a little distance away and give her a chance to concentrate. We got that fire pit over by the bunkhouse and some mesquite stacked up near it. I say let's have us a barbecue while we're waitin' for this baby to get born."

"Yeah!" Kyle said. "That would be great!"

"Wonderful idea," Leigh said with a smile. "An old-fashioned cowboy camp fire."

"I'll go start the fire," Duane said, sauntering off.

"And I'll run up to the house and get the steaks and the beans," Ry offered, heading for Freddy's pickup.

"This will be fun." Leigh turned to the cowhand named Davis. "How about fetching your guitar?"

Davis hoisted his belt over his large belly. "I can do that."

"Do you know any Lionel Richie songs? My mare is partial to *Penny Lover.*"

Davis looked offended. "Lionel Richie is not a country singer, ma'am."

"Just thought I'd ask," Leigh said with a chuckle.

By the time the sunlight faded from the sky, everyone except Leigh and Freddy were gathered around the fire. Ry slapped a few steaks on a huge metal grate and Duane stirred beans in a cast-iron pot. Beer and soda cans were passed around, and fat chunks of wood were pulled around the camp fire for seats. Joe remained standing next to Ry while he nursed a beer and kept an eye on the corral. And on Leigh, he admitted to himself.

Freddy walked over, looped an affectionate arm around Ry's waist and tucked her hand in his back pocket. "Leigh suggested we take fifteen-minute shifts watching Penny Lover. She's on the first watch, and Duane will be the second. I think Penny Lover did need a little more privacy than we were giving her. She seems much calmer now."

"I'll take a shift," Kyle volunteered.

"Maybe you'd like to come along on my shift," Freddy suggested. "I'm after Duane."

"Sure!" Kyle said happily. "You know what this is like, with everybody together? The crew of the *Enterprise*."

Freddy smiled. "I guess it is, at that. And our mission tonight is to bring a foal into the world."

Joe silently blessed her for agreeing with Kyle so easily. "Can I get you something to drink, Freddy?" he asked.

"A ginger ale would be great, thanks." She smiled at him, but there was a wariness in her eyes. She obviously hadn't forgotten that he considered her a suspect in the sabotage case.

Walking over to the ice chest to get Freddy's soda, he wished he could forget all the lessons he'd learned in his twenty years of being a cop. But perpetrators of crimes were seldom complete strangers, and this case had all the earmarks of an inside job. Yet, as he walked back into the firelit circle and looked around, it seemed impossible that anyone sitting there sharing a meal and swapping sto-

ries could be guilty of stampeding herds, setting brush-
fires and dynamiting dams.

Duane walked over and helped himself to some more
beans from the pot. "Ain't this like old times, Freddy?"
he asked.

"Yes, it is," she agreed. "A scene like this would have
made Thaddeus and Clara Singleton proud, after all the
things they went through a hundred years ago to keep
this place going."

"What things?" Kyle asked with his mouth full.

"The Apache Indians tried to wipe them out once,"
Freddy said.

"Really?" Kyle's eyes grew wide.

"And then, there was a summer when it didn't rain
much, and most of their herd died. There were some terrible dust storms, too."

"How do you know?" Kyle asked.

"Lots of people kept diaries in those days," Freddy told
him. "Leigh and I have Clara's, and another one written
by Clara's daughter-in-law, Ellie. After that generation,
we don't have as much—a few letters, some scrap-
books."

Kyle chewed thoughtfully. "I'd like to see them."

"I'll show them to you tomorrow," Freddy promised.
"Hey, Davis, how about a song?"

"You bet." The paunchy cowboy strummed a few experimental chords on his guitar and began "The Streets
of Laredo." Curtis and Rusty joined in, and Duane sang
along until he had to leave for his shift with Penny Lover.

By the time Leigh arrived in the circle, Davis had
switched to "Red River, Valley," a song about a woman
who was leaving the valley and taking the sunshine with
her. Joe thought of what this valley would be like with
the True Love gone. And Leigh gone. Unimaginable.

He levered himself to his feet and went over to take the tin plate she held in her hand. "Go relax. I'll get you something to eat. I assume you're just having beans and bread."

"And a beer?" she added with a grin.

Joe touched the brim of his hat. "Sure thing, ma'am."

"I do love a polite cowboy," she said, and walked over to sit on a stump beside Kyle.

The casual statement hit him with unexpected force. He didn't want her to be casual with a word like that. Not around him. He wanted her to save a word like that for...what? God, he was getting muddled.

He returned with her food and beer and sat quietly on Kyle's other side while she talked with Ry and Freddy. Then she coaxed Kyle into singing along when Davis launched into "Drifting Along with the Tumbling Tumbleweeds." And with her every smile, her every gesture, the ache in Joe's heart grew. He couldn't figure out what in the hell was wrong with him. Indigestion, most likely.

Eventually, Freddy glanced at her watch and handed her plate to Ry. "Your turn to do the dishes, darling. Kyle and I are due over at the corral for our shift." She motioned to Kyle. "Let's go, buckaroo."

Joe gazed after them. "That kid is having a ball."

Ry nodded. "I'll bet after tonight he's not going to want to go back with your friend Pope."

"He's most definitely not my friend."

Leigh set her plate on the ground. "Is he within his rights to drag Kyle back to New York?"

"He might be if he can prove negligence." Joe finished the last of his beer and crushed the can in his fist. "The thing that worries me is that he'd like to adopt Kyle and get me out of the picture completely. Somebody who knows the law as well as he does can be dangerous."

Ry clapped a hand on Joe's shoulder. "Don't worry. We can handle him." His eyes gleamed with anticipation. "And after that remark he made about going into town for a 'decent meal,' I'd take pleasure in fixing his little red wagon."

"That makes two of us."

"Three of us," Leigh said. When Joe looked at her in surprise, she winked at him. "Ain't it great to have friends, cowboy?"

"Yes, it is," he said, amazed at how much he meant it.

"Daddy!" Kyle called, running from the corral so fast he nearly tripped. "Daddy, it's time!"

Leigh jumped up, her face luminous, and walked quickly toward the corral. Everyone else around the circle deposited plates, cups and beer cans on the ground and followed her. When she started through the gate, she glanced at Kyle hopping along right beside her. Crouching, she took him by the shoulders and looked into his eyes.

Joe couldn't hear what she said, but Kyle nodded and climbed the fence to his perch on the top rail. Joe found a spot next to him and looked into the corral. "All ready for this, buddy?" he asked, putting an arm around Kyle's waist.

Kyle nodded, his face tight with excitement. "I can't be down there right now, because it's very tricky, but I get to *name* the baby when it's born."

"Hey, that's great." Joe gave him a hug. Then he stared in fascination at what was taking place in the corral. The Appaloosa remained standing while two forelegs and a head encased in what looked like blue plastic poked out. Joe concluded that horses and humans had a slightly different way of giving birth. As the birth progressed, Leigh stationed herself at Penny Lover's head and talked gently to her, while Freddy monitored the foal's progress.

"Leigh knows what that horse is thinking," Kyle said in a low voice.

Next to Kyle, Duane chuckled. "She's thinkin' she'd like to get this business over with."

As if to demonstrate the fact, Penny Lover dropped to her knees, and with a grunt rolled to her side.

Kyle gripped Joe's hand and spoke in an urgent whisper. "Here it comes. See, Daddy? Look, there it is!"

Sure enough, as Penny Lover heaved and snorted, the foal emerged, the placenta shimmering in the floodlight illuminating the corral. A muted cheer went up from the group leaning on the fence.

Freddy cleared the mucus from the foal's nose and peered at the foal's underbelly. Then she turned to Leigh with a triumphant smile. "It's a filly. A fine little filly. Let's stand back and let Penny Lover clean her baby."

Leigh leaned down and hugged Penny Lover around the neck before rising and backing away from mare and foal. Her shoulders quivered and she wiped her eyes with the back of her sleeve.

*She's crying,* Joe thought, *just like I did.* A lump formed in his throat, and he would have given anything to hold Leigh at that moment.

"I knew I should have ordered cigars," Ry mumbled, and his voice sounded suspiciously husky.

Penny Lover whinnied and turned to her baby. With great swipes of her tongue she cleaned the foal, and as the damp coat became more and more visible, Leigh reached out and gripped Freddy's arm. The little filly's rump was spotted with white, just like her mother's, just as Leigh had hoped, Joe remembered.

As a breathless audience watched, the mare stood and nudged her baby. The filly put her two impossibly long legs in front of her, lunged forward and toppled over. The group let out a collective sigh. She tried again, this time getting her hind legs under her for an instant before tumbling to the dirt again.

"She'll make it this time," Kyle announced.

And she did.

There was much chuckling and backslapping among the hands as the filly staggered toward her mother and began to nurse. Freddy and Leigh hugged and turned back toward the fence where Kyle, Joe and Ry waited.

"Well, Kyle?" Leigh asked, lifting her tear-stained face toward him. "What's her name?"

Kyle didn't hesitate. "Spilled Milk!"

Leigh nodded with satisfaction. "Perfect. Good thing she had the Appaloosa markings, though."

"I knew she would," Kyle said.

Leigh stuck her hands in her back pockets and gazed at him. "Learning how to read minds, buckaroo?"

Kyle grinned at her. "Could be."

# 11

LEIGH AND FREDDY needed to stay at the corrals with Penny Lover a while longer, but Joe could tell from Kyle's wide yawns that he was ready for bed. Kyle was finally persuaded to leave with Joe and Ry after Leigh promised him he could spend the next morning with Penny Lover and Spilled Milk.

Joe and Kyle rode with Ry in the van back up to the ranch house. Kyle kept drifting to sleep in the back seat, but then he'd rouse himself to talk about the birth of the foal one more time.

As Ry pulled into the parking area, Kyle suddenly jerked fully awake. "Oh, no! He was supposed to take me back tomorrow."

Joe knew exactly who Kyle meant. "Do you want to stay?" he asked quietly.

"Of course I do! Leigh told me I could go see Penny Lover and Spilled Milk. I like being a cowboy. I want to stay here with you, Dad. I have to stay. I just have to." Kyle sounded ready to cry.

"Then you will," Joe said, glancing over at Ry. Ry nodded.

Kyle swallowed noisily, as if fighting the tears. "But he said—"

"Never mind what he said." Joe turned in his seat to look at Kyle. "I'll find out where he's staying and call him. You won't have to go back."

Kyle sighed. "Thanks, Dad. You're the best."

"So are you, son."

Kyle's responding smile lit up the night.

Later, while Kyle got ready for bed, Joe picked up the bedside phone and put in a call to the golf resort where Pope was staying. Pope sounded wary when Joe identified himself.

"I'm afraid you made the trip for nothing," Joe said. "Kyle wants to stay a few more days."

"That's unfortunate, because I'm taking him back tomorrow."

Joe longed to issue his own ultimatum, but he remembered Leigh's approach and decided to adopt it. "He learned quite a bit watching the foal being born tonight. Leigh, our head wrangler, has promised him he'll be able to spend a lot of time with the mare and filly. It's like a minicourse in biology."

Pope seemed to be mulling that over. "Darlene wants him home. She's really worried about him."

Kyle was in the bathroom brushing his teeth, but Joe lowered his voice, to be on the safe side. "Look, Pope, the kid's never even had a dog, and he was allowed to name this filly. You should have seen his face. It's as close to having his own animal as he may ever get. Don't take this away from him. He's safe. You have my word on that."

"Let me talk to Darlene and get back to you."

"Okay." Joe hung up the phone and prayed for patience.

"What did he say?" Kyle asked, coming into the room dressed in his Star Trek pajamas, a ring of toothpaste around his mouth.

"He's checking with your mother."

Kyle nodded. "He always does that."

"Really?"

**Vicki Lewis Thompson**     137

"He's always asking her, 'Should I wear this tie or that tie? Should I take them to lunch at this place or that place?' Stuff like that."

Joe worked up his courage to ask a question he'd never dared voice before. "What do you think of him?"

"Of Em?" Kyle shrugged. "He's okay, I guess, but he'd never make it on the *Enterprise*."

Joe bit back a smile. "Why not? He's smart."

"In some things, but when stuff goes wrong, like the time one of the apartments in our building had a fire, he gets all goofy and runs around in circles, screaming. Mom has to take over."

"Good thing somebody does." Joe never thought he'd be grateful for Darlene's bossy attitude, but at least she could handle a crisis. He was also beginning to suspect the real culprit behind the move to legally adopt Kyle. All along he'd thought it was Pope's idea.

The bedside phone rang and he picked it up. "Gilardini."

"Do you always have to answer the phone as if you were on a police radio?" Darlene asked.

"Hello, Darlene, nice to hear from you." Joe couldn't keep the sarcasm from his voice. Theirs had not been an easy divorce.

"I'm tempted to come out there myself and make sure Kyle's all right."

Joe squeezed his eyes shut and prayed.

"But as long as Emerson's there, and I'm in the middle of a project at work, I'll let him handle it."

Joe let out his breath. "Kyle's fine, Darlene. We got off to a rough start, but he won't be in any more dangerous situations. He wants to stay and get to know this little filly. It's a great opportunity."

"Let me speak to him."

Joe handed the phone to Kyle. The conversation was mostly on Darlene's side, and Joe suspected she was giving him a list of things to be afraid of. Joe looked away and gained control of his anger so that he wouldn't display it to Kyle.

"I miss you, too," Kyle said at last. "Want to speak to Dad again?" He paused. "Okay, 'bye," he said and replaced the receiver in the cradle. "I can stay." He didn't sound too jubilant about it.

"And?"

"And Em's staying, too. He's still going to be at that resort, but he'll be driving out every day to keep an eye on me." Kyle glanced at his father. "And you."

Joe groaned.

"Mom said he was an equestrian in college, so he's supposed to teach me the correct way to ride."

Joe gazed at Kyle and digested the news. "An equestrian?"

"You know, somebody who rides—"

"I know what the word means." A small smile crept over his lips. "And I hope he announces it just that way to the folks down at the corrals tomorrow morning."

DUANE FINALLY CONVINCED Freddy and Leigh that Penny Lover could handle her baby without people hovering around the corral all night.

"I'm so glad we decided to breed her, even if the stud money was hard to justify when we were struggling last year," Leigh said to Freddy as they pulled up in front of the ranch house.

"Me, too." Freddy shut off the engine and sat gazing at the house, its windows spilling light onto the porch. "That little filly seems like a sign that everything is going to work out. Joe's going to find out who's sabotaging the ranch and he's also going to agree we shouldn't sell it to developers."

"I want to believe that, too. But I should warn you, he has his emotions locked in a vault. He's not the sort to be swayed by sentimentality about the old homestead."

Freddy looked at her. "But he *has* emotions, I assume?"

Leigh thought of the restrained power of his kisses. "Yes."

"If anybody can dig them out, you can, baby sister."

"I'm almost afraid to try. The result could be something like the flash flood after the dam was dynamited. People could be swept away."

Freddy contemplated her for a long moment. "But isn't that what you've been waiting for? A great passion destined by the stars?"

Leigh swallowed. "Theoretically. In practice, it's scary as hell."

"All these years you've been telling me you couldn't get serious about this one or that one because he wasn't the explosive lover who could fulfill your destiny. Are you saying that Joe could be that lover, and you're backing away?"

"You don't understand." Leigh's voice dropped to a whisper. "He has the power to break me."

Freddy reached over and squeezed her knee. "The best ones all do, sweetie. Take my word, they're worth the risk. And speaking of that, I'm going inside and commune with that special guy of mine."

Leigh opened her door. "Remember how Dad used to drive out to the homestead every time a foal was born and take a bottle of champagne?"

"I do." Freddy climbed down and started toward the house.

Leigh fell into step beside her. "I bought some champagne last week. I'm going out there and thank Clara and Thaddeus for the gift of Spilled Milk."

"Great idea. I'd join you, but now that I'm expecting, champagne's off limits. And—"

"You need to be with Ry," Leigh finished. "That's okay. I have some thinking to do, anyway." She followed Freddy through the front door and nearly collided with Joe.

"I thought I saw you two drive up," he said. "Listen, I wanted to thank you for... well, everything. Kyle will remember watching that foal being born for the rest of his life. And getting to name her, too.... It was the best thing you could have done for him."

Freddy's glance flicked between them. "Where is the little buckaroo?"

"Sound asleep, with a big smile on his face."

Freddy nodded. "That's nice. Leigh was headed out to the old homestead to drink a bottle of champagne in celebration," she added casually.

"I see. Well, I wouldn't want to hold you up. I just wanted to thank you for giving Kyle such a great experience."

Freddy shot a look at her sister. "Yes, well, we took a big *risk* breeding Penny Lover, but the *reward* was certainly worth it, wasn't it, Leigh?"

Leigh wasn't sure if Freddy had forced the issue, or if the evening was unfolding in an inevitable pattern. Whatever the explanation, this was a crossroads she would have reached sooner or later, with or without Freddy's intervention. Perhaps it was appropriate she face this challenge after receiving the gift of Penny Lover's foal. The universe didn't reward cowards.

Taking a deep breath, she looked up at Joe. "Would you like to drive out to the homestead with me and share the champagne?"

Momentary surprise was soon replaced by a soft glow of awareness in his gray eyes. "Yes."

"I'll go get the champagne from the kitchen, then."

"I'll be here," he said as Freddy and Leigh walked away.

Freddy waited until they were through the swinging kitchen door before she let out a muffled whoop of triumph.

"It's all your fault," Leigh said. "If this turns out to be a rotten idea, I'm going to haunt you to the end of your days, Frederica Singleton McGuinnes."

"Where's your ability to see into the future? You should be able to tell how things will turn out."

"The only way I can do that is when my mind is completely relaxed. When I'm around that man, my mind is anything *but* relaxed."

Freddy grinned. "I've been waiting for this day for years. Now go get the champagne and wait right here. I'll be back in a minute."

Leigh retrieved her bottle from the walk-in food locker and plucked two champagne flutes from a shelf. As she turned from the glassware cupboard, Freddy reappeared from the hallway that led to the private wing of the house.

"Tuck these in your pocket." She thrust several small cellophane packages at Leigh.

"Oh, for heaven's sake!"

"Take them! A man on a vacation with his son should not be expected to carry birth control around with him."

"Freddy, we probably won't even—"

"Then you can bring them back, can't you? Here." Freddy shoved them into Leigh's pocket.

"What if he finds them? How will I explain the fact that I'm running around with condoms, as if I expected something to happen?"

Freddy smiled. "If he finds them, it will be because something is about to happen. Now, go."

So that was how Leigh happened to be driving out to the old homestead site with a bottle of champagne, two crystal flutes and a pocketful of condoms. Next to her loomed a man who seemed to take up more space than she remembered. He held the flutes in one big hand, the champagne bottle in the other. Every time she reached for the floor shift on the old truck, her hand came dangerously close to his knee. When the truck bounced over a rut, his arm brushed hers. The truck cab filled with the masculine, spicy scent of him, and her heart wouldn't behave.

Compared with Joe, the men she'd dated seemed immature and boring. His profession might have closed off his more tender emotions, but it had also surrounded him with an irresistible cloak of valor. He was a modern-day knight in armor, a protector of those smaller and weaker than himself. His presence made her nervous, yet expectant.

"My father started this custom," she said as the headlights picked out the rutted road in front of them. "He called it 'A Toast to the Ghosts.' Every time a foal was born, he drove out here with a bottle of champagne. My mother was sure he would run himself into a tree on the way back, but he never did."

"Did he drink the champagne sitting on the concrete floor?"

"No, he sat in the back of the truck. That way, he didn't have to worry about snakes while he was celebrating."

"Sounds like an interesting man."

"He was a Singleton," Leigh said. "They've been known for doing things their way."

"So I've noticed."

Leigh pulled into the clearing where the concrete slab gleamed a pale white in the light from the stars. "Well, here we are." The beating of her heart sounded loud in her ears. "I guess we could just sit in the cab and drink the champagne."

"That isn't what your father would have done."

"No, he liked to be able to look up at the stars while he contemplated his good fortune."

Joe opened the door. "Then let's go."

The next few minutes were filled with the business of getting situated. The truck bed was littered with an inch or so of hay left over from the time Leigh had hauled a couple of bales out to Duane's herd. Joe set down the champagne and glasses while he helped her spread an old blanket over the hay. It felt for all the world as if they were making up a bed with fresh linens, and then climbing into it as they settled themselves on the blanket, took off their hats and leaned against the cab. Down in the riverbed, a pack of coyotes yipped and barked as they chased a rabbit. Without a moon, the stars were so thick they looked like a dusting of powdered sugar.

"I feel as if I should take off my boots," Joe said.

Leigh's pulse quickened, and she took a steadying breath. "Go ahead."

As he leaned down and did exactly that, she threw caution to the winds and took hers off, too, while he opened the bottle. She was impressed with how well he knew his way around a champagne cork.

After he'd poured them each a glass, he sat the bottle beside him and raised his goblet. "To Spilled Milk."

"To Spilled Milk, my wonderful little filly, appropriately born under Leo, sign of royalty." She clicked her glass against his and the chime carried through the clear air.

After they drank, Joe lifted his goblet again. "And to the Singleton nerve."

She touched her glass to his and met his penetrating gaze. "To the Singleton nerve." Then she closed her eyes and took a bigger swallow of champagne. Sometimes the Singleton nerve needed a little help. She settled back against the cab of the truck.

Joe followed suit, his shoulder brushing hers. "You had to think about it before you asked me out here tonight."

"A little."

"Why did you ask me?"

She drank some more champagne before answering. "To seduce you so you won't sell the True Love."

Joe's chuckle was warm and rich.

"What's so funny about that? Are you one of those untouchable cops who can't be bribed?"

"I answered that the other day, if you'll recall. When it comes to you, I'm very touchable."

A shiver of awareness ran up her spine. "So why did you laugh?"

"Because you wouldn't try to bribe me with sexual favors if your life, or even the ranch, depended on it. It's not in your nature."

"How can you be so sure? Didn't anybody tell you I'm descended from a lady of the night?"

Joe laughed again. "No, I can't say they did. Which ancestor was that?"

"Clara Singleton, wife of Thaddeus, the better half of the couple we're honoring here tonight."

"Clara was a prostitute?"

"There's good evidence she was, before she met Thaddeus. But you see, he was a very liberal-minded fellow, and he didn't care who had gone before him, so long as Clara pledged her love to him from that day forward. From reading her diary, I can tell she worshiped Thaddeus for restoring her good name." She took another sip of champagne. "She would have done anything for him."

"Sounds as if Thaddeus knew a good deal when he found one." He reached for her glass and refilled it. Their fingers brushed as he returned the glass to her. The contact was enough to interrupt the pattern of her breathing, but he didn't follow the gentle touch with anything more than a smile.

The champagne was making her reckless. "It was a good deal for him." She took a sip while still maintaining eye contact with Joe. "She wasn't an inexperienced virgin, like most of the brides he might have chosen. From a careful reading of the diary you can tell that Clara knew a lot about making love, and she taught Thaddeus everything she knew."

Desire flared in his eyes, but his voice remained calm. "Interesting." He drank his champagne, but his gaze never left hers. "So getting back to your original statement, you're telling me that you, a descendant of a former prostitute, have the ancestral background to use sex to get what you want. Does that about sum up your reason for asking me out here tonight?"

"It could."

"But it doesn't."

She gulped the last of her champagne.

He took the glass gently from her. "You don't need that to deal with me."

"Oh, yes, I do. I wouldn't mind having the rest of the bottle. I wouldn't mind being totally pie-eyed to deal with you, Officer Gilardini."

He put down his own glass and turned back to her. "Then let's see how you're progressing toward your goal." Rising to his knees, he cupped her elbows and drew her up to face him.

"What are you doing?"

"Administering a field test for sobriety."

"You're going to see if I can walk a straight line on my knees?"

His mustache twitched in amusement. "If you can do that, drunk or sober, we ought to get you on Letterman." He held up his index finger. "Follow the movement of my finger."

"Why?"

He sighed. "I knew you'd be a difficult test subject. This is called horizontal-gaze nystagmus. Now just do it."

She laughed but did as he asked.

"Mmm. Again."

She repeated the exercise.

Moving slowly, he cupped her face in both hands. "I regret to inform you that you are not intoxicated."

*Yes, I am.* "How could you tell?"

He caressed her cheeks with his thumbs, sending heat coursing through her. "If you had been, your eyes would have jerked involuntarily while you were following the movement of my finger. Yours didn't." His voice grew husky. "They're also the most luminous brown eyes I've ever tested."

Leigh gulped. "I think I need more champagne."

His voice was gentle but firm as he leaned toward her. "No, you don't," he murmured, holding her captive with the pressure of his fingers. "You're a Singleton." His mouth hovered above hers. "You can take the heat."

# 12

JOE KNEW he could be kissing a felon, and it showed how far gone he was that he no longer cared. If Leigh had hired someone to cause the accidents, she'd certainly lost control of the process. If it turned out she was implicated, he'd use everything he'd learned about the law to get her off. Maybe she was guilty of loving the ranch a little too passionately for her own good. Joe understood. It was the same sort of desperate need he was beginning to feel for her.

Her mouth opened beneath his as he'd known it would. She could no more deny him than he could deny her. He took her surrender with a fierce joy, thrusting his tongue deep into her sweetness as he pulled her close. He sought to ease the pounding demand of his body against the softness of her breasts, the valley between her thighs—ah.

Yet she was not close enough. He needed...needed... He opened her blouse, unfastened her bra and groaned with satisfaction as the unbound swell of her breast filled his cupped hand. She arched her back and he pushed the garments from her shoulders, baring her to the glow of starlight. It was her element. Surrounded by the silver glow, she lost all hesitancy and met his gaze with a passion that made him catch his breath in wonder.

He stared at her, dazzled as if confronted by a goddess. His voice rasped in the night. "Who are you, Leigh?"

"The one you came to find."

He shook his head. "But I didn't—"

"Didn't you?"

And he knew then that it hadn't been the ranch or the Old West he'd been seeking. It had been himself, the man he'd lost somewhere on the streets of the city. With this woman, he could be that man.

She reached for his hand, turned it palm up and feathered a kiss there. Then she placed it over her breast so he could feel her pounding heart, beating as rapidly as his. "I am flesh and blood, as you are, and our bodies have a powerful need for each other. But our spirits crave connection even more."

And he knew that, too. He'd known it from the moment he'd first looked into her eyes. He'd been fighting the knowledge because it didn't fit with anything he'd ever believed. But he couldn't deny what his trembling soul told him was true.

She brought his hand back to her mouth and kissed each finger before holding the back of his hand against her cheek. "Make love to me, Joe."

The deepest sorrow he'd ever felt washed over him. He hadn't expected this, not really. Even if he had, there'd been no time to make preparations. And no matter how unearthly the connection between them, it could have earthly consequences. He shook his head.

She released his hand and he mentally prepared himself to climb into the truck cab and ride back to the ranch for a long, agonizing night of abstinence. Instead, she smiled her enigmatic smile and reached into her pocket to withdraw several familiar-looking packets. "Would these help?"

He broke out laughing, a joyous sound that welled up from deep within him. "You are amazing. From fantasy to reality in the blink of an eye."

"Well?"

"Yes, these will help." He scooped them from her hand and tossed them to one side, right where he could find them again. Then he reached for her, holding her close as he gazed into her wondrous eyes. "And I *will* make love to you, Leigh Singleton," he murmured. "And count myself the luckiest of mortals to be allowed that."

She took his face in her hands. "I knew there was a poet in there somewhere."

"You would make a poet out of a stick of wood," he said, leaning down to drink nectar from her lips.

She unfastened his shirt, and he grew dizzy with the first contact of his skin against hers. Were there sparks from the friction, or was it desire exploding behind his eyes like Roman candles? He buried his face against her neck and the scent was of jungles he'd never seen, opulent flowers he'd never touched, yet he knew them as intimately as he would soon know her.

Her skin tasted like spice from the Orient, fruit from a tropical paradise, ambrosia from the depths of his fantasies. She created a world in the circle of her arms and offered it to him. Offered. Never had there been a sweeter word to describe the way she lifted her breasts for his pleasure. And he took shamelessly.

It was not enough. He removed the rest of her clothing that he might touch her essence, know the richness of her craving to be loved. She was lush with need, ripe for him, pulsing with his rhythm. He eased her back on the rough blanket, having only a moment to wish it could be velvet against her soft skin. But overwhelming awe swept away that mild regret as he gazed at her flawless body stretched beneath him.

Her image would be with him forever, yet he stroked her with the fervor of a blind man striving to memorize every nuance with his fingertips. She rewarded his touch with small gasps and moans that tightened his groin until he could stand no more and fought to free himself of his own remaining garments.

Looking into her bottomless eyes, he knew he could have slid effortlessly into her without thought of protection and she would not have resisted. The temptation flavored his tongue and trembled through his taut body, but he curbed it and reached for one of the packets beside her head. Distracted by the tumbled locks of her golden hair, he paused to comb his fingers through them. Then he opened the packet.

She watched him, her lips parted and her breath coming in quick spurts that made her breasts quiver. He leaned down to kiss those trembling peaks, to draw them once more into his mouth and feel the excruciating pleasure against his tongue. Her small, inarticulate cries heated his blood and filled him with visions of burying himself deep within her. He released her and sheathed himself with unsteady movements.

When he glanced back at her, his breath caught in his chest. She opened her arms, opened her thighs in a gesture of giving so complete that he moaned in ecstasy. He moved over her, knowing that he would never be the same man from the moment he joined with this woman. He held her gaze as he moved slowly, taking his time, entering her with the reverence due the most shattering moment of his life.

At last he was there, and she lifted her hand to trace the tears dampening his cheeks.

"Yes," she whispered in sweet benediction. Then she tightened around him, awakening the wildness that lay just beneath the surface.

With a sound deep in his throat that he barely recognized as his own, he drew back and thrust forward again. She rose to meet him with a gasp of approbation. He moved again, watching the light flare in her eyes. He worked with that light, building it into a bonfire that made her body glisten in the starlight. In this moment he would claim what she had offered. And she would no longer be the same woman who lay down beneath him.

Surging within her, he lost all sense of where he left off and she began. Nothing mattered but the entity they were creating together, a fusion born of white-hot heat and primitive rhythms. At the moment she arched and cried out, synergy pulled him into the same spiral of release, and he surrendered as never before, without fear, spinning through time and space, his soul entwined with hers.

THE RISKS OF HEARTBREAK remained the same, but now Leigh had savored the rewards and knew she would dare anything to hold this man in her arms. For a few precious moments, he'd cast aside his protective armor and allowed her a glimpse of the richness of emotion he kept hidden like a casket of stolen jewels. No matter how he closed himself off again, he could never take back the naked passion that blazed in his eyes as he rose over her, or the tears when he claimed her.

He stirred and lifted his head from where he'd nestled in the curve of her shoulder. He gazed into her eyes and his mustache lifted as he gave her a slow smile. "Have we landed yet?" he asked softly.

"We may never touch earth again."

He brushed his lips against hers, tickling her with his mustache. "I don't know astrology from Astroturf, but something weird is going on here."

She nibbled on his lower lip. "People don't always have to believe in things for the consequences to affect them. But in case you're interested, we called down some mighty forces tonight."

"I'd be a fool not to agree with you." He touched his forehead to hers. "I've never had an experience even close to that."

"Of course not. Neither have I."

"Because it's written in the stars?"

"That's right."

"This requires some thinking." He eased away from her and reached for the edge of the blanket. Then he pulled it over both of them as he rolled slowly to his back and gazed up at the spangled sky. "You believe what happened tonight between us was predestined?"

At least he was no longer making fun of the idea, she thought. "What other explanation can you give? You were in an elevator accident, a rare thing in itself, right?"

"Almost never happens these days."

"And you met Ry McGuinnes, who happened to be interested in buying this ranch."

"And I came out here and saw you." He reached for her hand beneath the blanket. "Then the fireworks started."

"And where is the first place we made love? The same place Clara and Thaddeus first made love."

He caressed her palm with his thumb. "You said she wasn't the virginal type, so they might have fooled around someplace else before he built this place."

"Nope. I've read Clara's diary. They didn't make love until their wedding night, when he carried her over the threshold of the adobe house he'd built for her, under the lintel with the True Love brand burned into it. She was very proud of that wedding night, almost as if the abstinence cleansed her of her past."

He lay quietly for a moment. Finally, he brought her hand to his lips and kissed it gently, tickling the back of it with his mustache. "I don't know if I can buy everything you're saying, but when I made love to you just now, I felt like that. It seemed like my first time, as if the other women I'd taken to bed were wiped out of my memory. Burned out, is more like it."

Leigh's chest tightened and tears blurred the clear light of the stars. "Yes."

His breathing quickened. "For you, too?"

"Yes."

He turned on his side and propped his head on his hand so he could look at her. He cupped her face and stared intently into her eyes. "That's wonderful to hear. You can't imagine how wonderful." He paused. "And I know what should come next now that you've confessed how you feel. But the thing is, you'd be getting a bum deal with someone like me."

Although she'd expected him to say something like that, it still made her heart trip and stumble. "I'm willing to accept the risk."

"I doubt you even know the extent of the risk."

"I—"

"Do you know why I decided to leave police work?"

"I suppose because you were sick of the violence."

He shook his head. "That's a good, standard answer, but it's not true. What many people don't realize is that a lot of cops get hooked on the excitement that violence brings, and I was one of them. Looking back, I'm not surprised Darlene left me. I was a terrible husband. Being around her bored me compared to being on the job.

Even Kyle's activities bored me, so I wasn't much of a father, either."

Secretly she'd feared this part of his personality, but she grasped at hope with both hands. "Yet you did quit the force. And you're trying to connect with Kyle."

"And making a mess of it, too." He sighed. "There was a time I was a lot like Kyle. But I killed off that part of myself when I was pretty young."

"No, you didn't." She reached up and stroked the soft line of his mustache. "I met that side of you tonight."

He looked down at her, longing darkening his gaze. "I don't want to hurt you," he murmured. "And I can be such a bastard sometimes."

"And an angel sometimes." She smiled. "I—"

He tensed and glanced out into the darkness.

She started to speak and he pressed a hand over her mouth. Then she heard the voice.

"Right there, you dummy!" came the harsh male whisper. "A dark blue pickup!"

She shivered as if someone had thrown ice water over her. Joe slowly extricated himself from the blanket and his hand closed over the neck of the champagne bottle.

"Nobody's in it," said another man.

"But somebody drove it out here," said the first speaker.

Leigh didn't recognize either voice.

She could feel the transformation in Joe. With stealthy movements, he reached for his clothes and put them on with an amazing lack of noise. Excitement radiated from him, and she remembered seeing him this way twice before—once when the bull had charged at him and then again when the dam had burst. So this was the demon within him she had to fight.

"I don't like it," said the first speaker. "Somebody's around. Let's go back."

"He won't be happy if we do," said the second man.

"Who gives a damn if he's happy? Come on."

Joe pulled on his boots too hastily, causing one heel to scrape against an exposed part of the truck bed.

"There!" said the first man. "Someone's here!" His exclamation was followed by the sound of boots scrambling against sand and rocks.

Joe leapt from the truck bed, the champagne bottle in his hand as he started in the direction of the running men.

Leigh peered into the shadows created by creosote bushes and cactus. Joe couldn't run through there without getting something stuck in him, but she knew better than to call out and tell him that. Then came the distinct thud of hooves pounding the desert floor. The men were escaping on horseback.

Soon afterward, Joe reappeared in the clearing and walked over to the truck bed. "They got away. Did you recognize either of the voices?"

"No."

"Where's your flashlight?"

"Under the seat, but the batteries are dead."

"What the hell good is a flashlight with dead batteries?" The question cracked like a whip in the still night.

"Nobody's made a trip into town to get fresh ones recently!" she retorted, struggling into her clothes. "My God, you sound as if having dead batteries were a crime."

"They could *cause* a crime. I can't believe you were willing to drive out here in the middle of the night without a working flashlight. There's a dangerous jerk on the loose somewhere on this ranch. What if I hadn't come with you?"

"I wouldn't have to listen to this tongue-lashing!"

"Every vehicle should have a working flashlight," he insisted stubbornly.

"Oh, stuff it, Officer Gilardini. I'll drive you to the ranch so you can pick up your working flashlight, since I'm sure you have one in that Chevy of yours. Then you can come back out here and prowl around to your heart's content, doing your cop thing."

They drove to the ranch in tense silence. When they reached it, she turned off the engine and left the keys in the ignition. "Take the truck when you go out again," she said. "Your Cavalier will bottom out on the ruts."

"Thanks."

Scooping up the champagne flutes from the seat, she opened her door and stepped down from the truck.

"I warned you," he said, opening his door.

She leaned her head against the cool metal of the door. "Yes, you did." She glanced up at him "Did you run into any cactus when you took off after them?"

He shrugged.

"You did, didn't you? I suppose you still have thorns in a few places. Let's go inside and I'll—"

"A few thorns won't kill me. I need to get back out there before anything gets disturbed."

"I'll go with you."

"No."

She sighed. "Yes, you did warn me, didn't you?"

He met her comment with silence. She turned and walked toward the house under stars that suddenly seemed cold and very far away.

EVEN WITH A FLASHLIGHT, Joe didn't find anything of value. The ground was too rocky to have recorded much in the way of footprints or hoofprints. A sophisticated crime lab might have been able to do something, but Ry didn't want Joe calling anyone in on the investigation. Used to dealing with a support system, Joe was discovering just what a hindrance working on his own could be. If only he could have caught one of those guys. Someone had sent them out to the homestead site, and he'd bet good money that the someone was the perp he was looking for. He wondered what the homestead had to do with it all.

Finally, he gave up and drove back to the dark ranch house. He wondered if Leigh was asleep. He doubted it, just as he doubted that he'd sleep much in the hours that were left of the night. He smacked the steering wheel in frustration. A lot of years had gone into making him the man he was. One night of lovemaking, no matter how terrific it had been, couldn't alter how he approached life, no matter how much she might wish it would.

FOR KYLE'S SAKE, Leigh exuded good cheer all through breakfast the next morning. To his credit, Joe made the same attempt. All three of them walked out the front door of the ranch house looking as if they were the best of friends. The falsity of it made Leigh's heart ache.

As they started to get into Leigh's truck for the trip to the corrals, Pope drove up in his rented BMW. He climbed from behind the wheel, and Leigh stared. "I believe we have a catalog cowboy on our hands," she muttered under her breath.

"A what?" Kyle asked.

"I'll explain later," she said.

Pope adjusted his white Stetson and walked toward them. Leigh hoped he'd think her smile came from friendliness and not amusement. It was hard to keep a straight face looking at that pristine white felt. Apparently, Pope hadn't heard that modern-day good guys wore black hats. He walked a little stiffly in his new jeans and didn't seem quite used to the heels on his boots. The boots alone would have attracted Leigh's complete attention, decorated as they were with bucking broncos in amazing shades of red, purple and green against a white background that was supposed to coordinate, she guessed, with the hat.

Joe propped his hands on his hips and gazed at Pope. Then he turned to Kyle. "I think your equestrian's here."

Kyle looked his stepfather over, from the tip of his outrageous boots to the crown of his white Stetson. "Guess so."

Leigh bit the inside of her cheek to keep from laughing. Kyle was definitely picking up a cowboy's gift for understatement.

"I'll take the boy with me," Pope said.

Joe nudged his hat to the back of his head. "I dunno. Looks like you might have trouble driving in that get-up."

"I would expect that sort of comment from you, Gilardini. Come on, Kyle."

Kyle looked to Joe for confirmation, and Leigh wondered if Joe would kick up a fuss. Instead, he nodded to his son and Kyle trooped off to the BMW with Pope.

Leigh and Joe got into the pickup and led the way to the corrals. "I was sure you'd insist that Kyle ride with us," she said as they started off.

"No use trying to hang a guy when he looks determined to hang himself. When I found out he was an equestrian, as he puts it, I decided to sit back and watch the fun."

"I hope that's what it turns out to be. To be honest, I don't look forward to putting up with him all morning."

"Probably not any more than you look forward to putting up with me."

She shot a glance in his direction. Dammit, no matter how much he frustrated and irritated her, he still had the power to twist her heart. She wanted to stop the truck, take that stubborn face in both hands and kiss that grim mouth until she connected with the passionate man who had loved her so well the night before.

"For what it's worth, I'm sorry," he said.

"For what?" Once before she'd leapt to a conclusion about his apology. She was determined not to do it again.

"For making an issue of the flashlight."

Her shoulders sagged in relief. "I thought you might be apologizing for making love to me."

"Not in a million years."

The statement squeezed the air from her lungs. "Does . . . that mean you might be interested in trying it again sometime?"

He groaned.

"Joe?"

"I can't believe you have to ask," he said softly.

"I was afraid that—"

"I would walk across hot coals to take you in my arms again, if you're fool enough to want me."

She gulped as desire pounded through her. "I guess I am that much of a fool." She parked the truck at the corrals and worked to control her trembling.

Joe covered her hand with his as she reached to turn off the ignition. Her gaze swung up to meet the intensity in his gray eyes. He didn't say anything, but he didn't have to. His longing and confusion were reflected there for her to read. She turned her hand over and laced her fingers through his. He gripped her hand tightly and the confusion gradually faded from his eyes. She smiled, and slowly, he smiled back.

"Let's go," she whispered. "We're keeping the equestrian waiting."

"Right." With a final squeeze, he released her.

# 13

JOE NOTICED that Pope and Kyle had already started toward Penny Lover's corral when he and Leigh left the truck. As Pope walked across the clearing, he collected stares and smirks from the cowboys he passed. Curtis was so busy watching Pope, he tossed a shovelful of manure down the front of Rusty's shirt.

Duane came out of the tack shed carrying a saddle and nearly dropped it when he saw Pope. "Who ya got there, Kyle?" he called when he recovered himself.

"This is my stepdad, Em," Kyle said.

"Glad to know ya," Duane said, his mustache twitching. "Thought for a second there it was Tom Mix hisself showed up at the True Love."

"I'm going to take him to see Spilled Milk," Kyle said.

"Then I'm going to show Kyle the correct procedure for riding a horse," Pope said. "I'd appreciate it if you'd saddle one for me."

"What type ya want?"

"Preferably one with spirit. I don't want some worn-out trail pony."

"Okeydoke." Duane nodded his head wisely. He stood and watched Kyle lead Pope away.

"What do you think of our new equestrian?" Leigh asked as she and Joe approached Duane.

"Is *that* what he is?" Duane spat into the dirt and hung the saddle over the hitching post. "I was wonderin'."

"How are mama and baby doing this morning?"

Duane's weathered face creased in a wide grin. "Them two made me plum glad to git up this mornin'. Penny Lover's given us a fine little filly. A fine little filly."

"Well, I'm going over for a visit," Leigh said. "Want to come with me, Joe?"

Joe felt like following her to the ends of the earth, but he had to use some discretion. "I'd just as soon wait until Pope clears out of that area, if you don't mind. I'm resolved not to punch the guy, but too much proximity and I might forget that resolve."

"Okay." She sauntered over to the far corral.

"Sweet on her, ain'tcha?" Duane asked.

Joe realized he'd been staring after Leigh and felt a flush creep up his neck as he glanced at Duane.

"Don't blame ya none. 'Scuse me. I have to call up to the house and check somethin' with Ry." He reappeared in less than three minutes. "Jist as I thought. Let's you and me go catch a couple of horses." He tossed Joe a bridle.

Joe was pleased that Duane thought him enough of a ranch hand to assign him a chore. "Which ones?"

"I'm gonna need Destiny so's I can work him some before the rodeo comin' up. You catch Red Devil for our equestrian over there."

"Red Devil? Ry's horse?"

"That's what I jist checked. Asked Ry if he thought Red Devil had enough spirit for this feller who had to stay at a resort last night to git a decent meal. Ry thought Red Devil would do nicely."

Joe grinned. "Isn't Red Devil kind of particular about who gets on him?"

"Yep."

By the time Leigh, Kyle and Pope came back, Joe and Duane had saddled Red Devil. Joe found a piece of straw to chew on, leaned against the rough adobe walls of the tack shed, tipped his hat lower over his eyes and prepared to enjoy himself.

Duane swung a saddle up on Destiny, the ranch's best cutting horse, before glancing at Pope. "That horse should suit ya," he said, tipping his head toward Red Devil.

Leigh raised an eyebrow in Duane's direction, but he pretended not to notice.

"Fine-looking animal." Pope adjusted his glasses and folded his arms."

"Jist go ahead and climb aboard," Duane said. "I got some things to do, but I'll be back to check on ya in a bit."

"No need. I want to put on a little demonstration for Kyle, here."

Duane swung up on Destiny. "Oh, I imagine you'll do that." He clucked to his horse and started around behind the tack shed.

Leigh put a hand on Kyle's shoulder. "Let's go over in the shade of the tack shed while your stepdad shows us what riding is all about."

"Okay." Kyle walked with her over to the shed. After glancing at his dad, he picked up a piece of straw, stuck it in the corner of his mouth and propped himself against the wall in exact imitation of Joe's stance, complete with one booted foot angled against the adobe.

When Kyle tugged his hat down over his eyes, Joe had to chuckle, but he was secretly thrilled that Kyle admired him enough to copy his behavior.

Pope seemed pleased to have an audience. He untied Red Devil's reins from the hitching post with a flourish and looped them over the animal's neck. Red Devil rolled his eyes and backed up a few steps.

"Whoa, there, big fella," Pope said, shuffling after him as he held the saddle horn.

"Did Ry okay this?" Leigh asked in a low voice.

"Absolutely." Joe realized with delight that Pope was planning to mount Red Devil on the wrong side. He also noticed that Curtis and Rusty were both leaning on their shovels to watch.

"You have to show them who's boss, Kyle," Pope said as he attempted to get his foot in the stirrup on the horse's right side. Red Devil tossed his head and sidled away. "I can see this horse needs to learn a few manners." Pope angled for the stirrup again, but Red Devil circled away from him and the stirrup twisted in his hand. Finally, Pope managed to shove his foot in, but Red Devil kept moving away from his intended rider, forcing Pope to hop after him in a circle, cursing under his breath. His cheek twitched as his tic started acting up.

Joe bit down on his straw to keep from laughing out loud. After a few moments, Pope grabbed the saddle horn and lunged upward. The stirrup untwisted and he landed in the saddle facing Red Devil's rump.

"Is that a trick or something, Em?" Kyle asked.

Joe almost choked on his piece of straw.

Red-faced, Pope managed to clamber down before Red Devil tossed him off, which required some agility, Joe had to admit. The big gelding pawed the ground and snorted menacingly while Pope muttered to himself.

"Comin' through," Duane called, riding out from behind the tack shed. He had a coiled rope in one hand as he casually herded Romeo into the clearing. Pope was concentrating on Red Devil and didn't notice what was coming up behind him.

Joe straightened and put a hand on Kyle's shoulder.

"It's okay," Leigh whispered, laying her hand on Kyle's other shoulder. "He's very tame without that bull rope on him."

"How're you doin'?" Duane asked Pope. "Thought you'd be on that horse by now."

"Nobody taught this bag of bones how to stand still," Pope said, starting to turn around. "I'd advise you to—"

Joe had always thought "his eyes bugged out of his head" was just an expression, but that was exactly what happened with Emerson J. Pope. Then he opened his mouth, but he didn't yell. He didn't even scream. He squeaked. Joe had never heard such a peculiar sound in his life. Pope dropped Red Devil's reins, turned tail and ran as fast as his new boots would carry him toward his rented BMW. His white hat flipped off and landed in the dirt, but he didn't go back for it.

As Joe, Leigh, Kyle, Duane, Curtis, Rusty and even Romeo watched in amazement, Pope spun the BMW in a dusty circle and bounced down the road going much faster over such rough terrain than the rental company would have appreciated.

Kyle shook his head. "He'd never make it on the *Enterprise*."

Joe felt a stab of remorse. Kyle had to live with this guy, jerk that he was, for some of the year, at least. He crouched next to his son and cleared his throat. "And most of the time, that doesn't matter. I'm sure the guy has his good points, too."

"Yeah." Kyle grinned. "But he sure is a dweeb, isn't he, Dad?"

"I'm afraid he is," Joe replied solemnly. "But dweeb or not, I'm going after him to smooth things over." He stood and glanced at Leigh. "Think Ry would mind if I borrowed his horse?"

"I'm sure he wouldn't," Leigh said, her brown gaze warm and encouraging.

Red Devil tossed his head around some, but Joe managed to get aboard. As he started away from the corrals, Kyle ran after him holding Pope's dust-covered hat. Joe leaned down and took it. "Thanks, buddy."

"I don't want him to take me home yet," Kyle said.

"I know. That's one reason I'm going after him."

"Thanks, Dad."

Joe touched the brim of his hat, and Kyle touched his. Then Joe nudged Red Devil into a trot. He figured Pope would drive straight back to the resort instead of going to the ranch house, so he cut through the desert to head him off at the ranch's entrance road. Red Devil was already agitated and seemed happy to pick up the pace. Lying low over the big horse's neck, Joe savored the thrill of the chase. But this time, he wouldn't be arresting someone at the end of it, he reminded himself. Worse yet, if he did his job right, he'd be making amends to a lawyer.

He saw the cloud of dust to his left and coaxed Red Devil into a dead run. Horse and rider came out on the road a hundred yards ahead of the car. Red Devil reared, which nearly tossed Joe in the dirt but managed to get Pope's attention. He braked the car and dust billowed everywhere.

Joe got Red Devil under control and dismounted, keeping the reins in one hand. Pope climbed warily from his car. They eyed each other for several long seconds.

"I'm sorry about what happened back there," Joe said at last as he fingered the brim of the white Stetson. "The bull's really tame, but you didn't know that. The ranch hands have a twisted sense of humor, I'm afraid."

Pope nodded. "Once I was out of there, I realized they were only taunting me because I'm from New York. Is that the same bull that came at you and Kyle?"

"Yeah. That time, they had him trussed up with something called a bull rope, and he was pretty ornery. Even so, the hands subdued him in seconds. The people on this ranch know what they're doing. I realize what you and Darlene think, but Kyle's probably as safe out here as he is in Manhattan."

"Are you going to be spending more time with him?"

The question caught Joe off guard. "What do you mean?"

"When Kyle called us, we got the impression you weren't around much. He said that you were out on some sort of investigation. Darlene and I decided it was the same old story, that you hauled him out here but you didn't plan to spend time with him. That's one of the main reasons I came out, to be truthful."

Joe longed to strike back with some comment about the irony of a lawyer's being truthful, but he thought of Kyle and restrained himself. "Yes, I'll be spending more time with my son," he said, allowing himself to emphasize the last part. "And while we're on the subject, what's this horse manure of you trying to adopt him?"

"Look, I know cops. Darlene didn't have to tell me about all the times you buried yourself in your work and acted as if she and Kyle didn't exist. I thought you might even be relieved to end the charade of trying to be a father."

Joe clamped his back teeth together to keep from commenting on that with all the four-letter words it deserved. "You thought wrong," he said, his voice deadly calm.

"Well, Gilardini, it just so happens I have revised my opinion recently. All the way down to the corrals, Kyle talked about how great it was being here at the ranch with you." He glanced back down the road he'd just driven in such haste, and sunlight glinted off the lens of his glasses. "Doesn't appeal to me in the least, but Kyle seems happy. That's the important thing. I asked Kyle how long he'd like to stay, and he said he didn't want to leave until school started. That gives you another three weeks with him, if you want them."

The idea of accepting favors from Emerson J. Pope didn't sit very well, but Joe realized that he was partially responsible for the situation turning out as it had. He hadn't been the best husband and father in the world, and now it was pay-up time. "I want them," he said.

"Good. Then I'll be flying out today. Can't understand what you like about this godforsaken country."

"It grows on you." Joe stepped forward. "Here's your hat."

"Ah, keep it. I imagine you could use a good hat. Yours looks a little battered, if you don't mind my saying so. You look more like one of your employees than an owner of the place."

"Thank you. You couldn't have given me a better compliment." Joe tossed the hat toward Pope and he caught it awkwardly. "But you keep the hat. It's not my size."

"I would have thought it would fit perfectly."

"Nope." Joe swung into the saddle. "Way too big. See you, Emerson." Joe touched the brim of his hat and galloped down the road so Pope wouldn't see the grin of triumph on his face. He'd managed to get in the last word, and that didn't often happen with a lawyer. Life was good.

As JOE APPROACHED the corrals, the sight that greeted him made him catch his breath. Leigh had taken Penny Lover out of her pen and was leading her around the clearing, with Spilled Milk following obediently behind. And on Penny Lover's bare back, holding a fistful of mane and looking pleased with himself, was Kyle.

"Hi, Dad," he called, waving. "We're a parade, see?"

"I see." His throat constricted as he realized what Leigh had accomplished by getting Kyle up on the mare all by himself. It was all part of a natural progression to rid him of his fears, and it was working. Another three weeks and Kyle would love the ranch every bit as much as Joe had hoped he would. All because of Leigh. Joe's heart swelled with an emotion he'd skittered away from most of his adult life. And for the first time in a long while, he allowed himself to feel it.

He walked Red Devil over to the hitching post, dismounted and tethered the horse. Patting him on the neck, he walked over to meet Leigh as she circled the clearing again. "Looking good," he said.

"Thanks." Her expression sent him messages that sped up his heartbeat.

"What did Em say?" Kyle asked.

Joe dropped back to walk beside Penny Lover. "He's heading home today, but he can see how much you like the True Love, so you can stay here until school starts, if you want."

"All right!" Kyle swiveled around to the foal ambling along behind. "Did you hear that, Milk?" He turned back to his father. "I call her Milk for short. It's easier."

"I'm all for taking the easy way."

"Three weeks," Kyle said. "Wow. Did you duke it out with him?"

Joe glanced up at his son in surprise. "Why would you think that?"

Kyle shrugged. "I know how mad he makes you. The way he talks and stuff."

"Well, I didn't hit him. And I won't. He's your step-father, and he cares about you. For that he deserves respect. From me and from you."

Kyle gazed at him and finally nodded. "Okay."

Leigh looked over her shoulder at them. "As long as Red Devil's saddled, how about if we round up Mikey and Pussywillow and go for a little ride?"

"Three horses?" Kyle asked.

"Sure," Leigh said, her tone nonchalant. "If you can ride Penny Lover with nothing to hold on to but a hunk of her mane, you can handle Mikey."

"Pussywillow's smaller," Kyle said. "How about her instead?"

"Okay. Pussywillow it is. I'll take Mikey."

Joe was ecstatic, but he took his cue from Leigh and didn't make a big deal of the decision as they put Penny Lover and Spilled Milk into their pen and then saddled Mikey and Pussywillow. Leigh helped Kyle into the saddle, and although he looked a little nervous, he picked up the reins and nudged the gray mare with his heels as they set off down the road toward the old homestead with Leigh in front, Kyle next and Joe bringing up the rear on Red Devil.

Joe checked for possible problems, but the sky was clear and the breeze almost nonexistent. Leigh held Mikey to a sedate walk and kept up a stream of chatter, turning constantly in her saddle to smile back at Kyle. As they approached the homestead, memories of the night before flooded through Joe. He wondered if Leigh was being affected in the same way. Maybe she'd brought them out here on purpose, to fire his imagination. As if he needed his imagination fired. One look at her in her formfitting jeans and he was a wild man. All he lacked was the opportunity to do something about it.

Leigh rode into the clearing and reined Mikey in a wide circle to head back in. "I think this is far enough for today," she said to Kyle. "How are you doing?"

"Good." Kyle sat straight and proud in the saddle. "It's not so scary. Can we go faster?"

"Next time." She glanced over at Joe. "How are you doing, cowboy?"

He caught the subtle teasing in her question. She knew good and well that being out here was bombarding him with images of their lovemaking. "I'm getting a little hot," he said.

Leigh chuckled. "That's an Easterner for you. Can't take the heat."

"Maybe that's because we haven't learned all the tricks for relieving it," he said.

"Then I'll have to teach you some." She winked at him before she started back down the road.

"What's that piece of paper over there?" Kyle asked.

Joe followed the direction of Kyle's pointing finger. Sure enough, a sheet of white paper was stuck on a cholla cactus. He knew for a fact it hadn't been there the night before when he'd searched the area, but a dust devil could have picked it off the ground and swirled it into the cactus after he'd left.

"I'll get it," Leigh offered. "No point in leaving litter out here." She rode over to the cholla and dismounted.

Pussywillow followed, and Kyle allowed her to go. Joe stayed back, not wanting to crowd the gray mare. Everything had gone beautifully, and he didn't want Pussywillow spooking over a piece of paper. He would have preferred Kyle on Mikey, but Kyle on any horse was a miracle, so he couldn't complain.

He watched Leigh lift the paper carefully away from the thorns. Something moved at her feet. He looked closer and saw a hairy spider crawling slowly toward her boot. It was easily as broad as his spread hand. He tensed, knowing what might happen if Kyle noticed. "Leigh, go ahead and get on your horse now," he said as easily as possible. "Come on, Kyle. I'll lead us back."

Too late. Kyle glanced down, and his scream tore through the air. Before it ended, Pussywillow had grabbed the bit and bolted toward the riverbed.

Joe dug in his heels and Red Devil lunged after the mare. "Hang on!" Joe yelled as Kyle lost a stirrup. "I'm coming!" The little boy bounced in the saddle as Pussywillow careered down the trail, but he stayed on. Joe thundered after him. He knew that when they reached the riverbank Pussywillow would leap the distance to the sandy bottom. Even an experienced rider could be thrown. Kyle would never make it.

Joe gauged the distance to the riverbed. Fifty yards, forty yards, thirty. He drew alongside, reached for Pussywillow's bridle, missed, reached again. Ten yards. He grabbed and held on, pulling back on Red Devil's reins at the same time. Both horses skidded to a stop, their haunches nearly touching the ground. Panting, Joe stared down at the drop-off into the riverbed right below them.

Then he turned to Kyle. His son sat with both hands still gripping the saddlehorn, his face as white as the piece of paper Leigh had dismounted to retrieve. Joe opened his mouth to tell Kyle he should never, *never* scream when he was riding a horse. Kyle swallowed, and tears filled his eyes. He looked as if he expected the rebuke Joe was about to deliver.

Joe took a deep breath. "You did good," he said, reaching across to grip Kyle's arm. "You stayed on."

## 14

*IT'S HAPPENING*, Leigh thought as she led the way back to the corrals. Before her eyes, Joe was emerging from his shell and casting away his need to control. She'd been astounded when he'd decided to go after Emerson Pope, yet it was the right thing to do and he'd apparently handled it beautifully. His attitude toward Kyle had undergone a change, too, judging from his behavior after the runaway. The old Joe would have berated Kyle for scaring the horse. Instead, father and son ended the episode with mutual respect.

The mood was lighthearted as they dismounted, unsaddled the horses and groomed them before turning them loose in the corrals. After a quick visit to Penny Lover and Spilled Milk, they decided to go up to the house for some lunch. Leigh had forgotten about the piece of paper she'd retrieved until she climbed into the driver's side of her truck and the paper crinkled in her back pocket.

She pulled it out and handed it to Joe. "Here's the thing that Kyle saw. I haven't even looked at it."

As they drove, Joe unfolded the paper and studied it. "This is a photocopy of a handwritten document. There's a date here. I think it's June, no, January, abbreviated. January—let's see—could be 1885."

Kyle leaned over to look. "Maybe it's a diary, like Leigh was telling us about last night."

"It reads like that," Joe said. "And it sounds like it was written by a prisoner of some sort. He mentions a guard, and working on a rock pile and taking exercise in the yard."

Leigh wondered if the diary page had anything to do with the men she and Joe had heard the night before, but her rendezvous with Joe wasn't a subject she intended to discuss in front of Kyle. "It could be from a college class," she said. "Students hike out here a lot. Maybe they were studying something from the time period when the ranch was homesteaded, and they dropped some of their papers."

"This is August," Joe said. "Is school in session?"

"I don't know. Maybe a summer class."

"Do you think it's a clue, Dad?" Kyle asked.

"Probably not." Joe folded the paper and snapped open his breast pocket to tuck it inside.

As they pulled up in front of the ranch house, Freddy and Dexter came down the flagstone walkway.

"I've left Ry to supervise construction on the rodeo arena and we're going into La Osa for ice cream," Freddy said. "Anybody want to come along?"

"Me!" Kyle said and started toward the ranch van.

"Hold it, buddy." Joe put out a restraining hand. "You haven't had lunch yet."

"I'll buy him a sandwich first," Freddy promised. "I'm sure Dexter would love it if Kyle came along."

"Yep," Dexter said.

"Okay. Sure," Joe said.

"Great!" Kyle ran over to Dexter and they exchanged high fives.

Joe snapped open his pocket. "Listen, while you're there, could you get a copy of this for me?" He handed her the diary page. "I don't know if it's important, but we found it out by the old homestead."

"Be glad to," Freddy said.

"What's that?" Dexter asked.

"A page from a diary," Kyle said. "I'll read it to you on the way to town, okay?"

"Good," Dexter said, nodding. "Let's go."

Leigh and Joe waved as Freddy, Dexter and Kyle drove off in the van. Then they turned toward each other, their eyes communicating the same silent message. Opportunity had just knocked.

Leigh tilted her head and gazed up at him, her pulse racing. "There's something I need to show you."

"Is that right?"

"One of our secret ways of relieving the heat around here."

"I'm partial to secrets."

"Then come with me." She led him around the side of the house to the back door that accessed the family wing. The prospect of loving him made her blood race, but there was no point in advertising their activities to the rest of the ranch. She suspected Freddy would guess. Freddy might even have suggested taking Kyle into La Osa on purpose. Bless her.

They ducked into the shade of a small porch and in through the back door. Leigh's room was on the end, next to Freddy and Ry's. With both her sister and brother-in-law out of the house, it was the most privacy she and Joe could hope for.

Inside the room she closed the door and pulled the shades, eliminating the rainbow colors flung by the crystals she hung there to catch the sunlight. Then she turned to find him surveying the room with interest. His gaze traveled to the unusual dream-catcher hanging above her headboard. The large webbed circle, at least eighteen inches across, contained a small crystal unicorn in the center. Peacock feathers hung from the edge of the circle.

"You have something like earrings like that," he said.

She nodded. "The legend says that bad dreams are trapped in the web, and good dreams are allowed to pass through."

"Does it work?"

"You're here."

Passion ignited in his eyes and he started toward her. She held up her hand. "Wait."

He paused, lifting his eyebrows in question.

"You'll see." She moved slowly around the room, reveling in his hot gaze as she lit jasmine incense, slipped a tape of soft synthesizer rhythms into the recorder and found the oils she needed. She'd spent years perfecting her massage techniques to relieve pain. She'd never used them to excite a man to unearthly desires. Joe would be the first.

She faced him. "Take off your clothes and lie on the bed. Relax and focus on your breathing while I'm gone."

He gave her a wry smile. "If I'm lying in your bed waiting for you, I doubt I'll be able to focus on my breathing."

"Try." She went into the adjoining bathroom, removed all her clothes and slipped on a white silk toga scented with the aroma of ripe raspberries. Her skin was flushed with anticipation, her nipples tight with desire. She had never brought a man here, to her sanctuary. She'd never allowed a man to touch that part of her being that danced with the powers of the universe. She had been waiting . . . for this man.

She returned to the room. He'd propped her pillows behind his head and lay watching her as she crossed to him. They'd made love in starlight before, and she hadn't seen him well. She knew there were scars—she'd felt the ridges and absorbed some of the stories they told. He lay against her snowy sheets, a magnificent warrior marked by battle, a man aroused by passion.

He noticed the sweep of her gaze. "It's the body of a street cop," he said.

"The body of a brave man."

"No."

She put one knee on the bed and leaned toward him to run a hand over his chest as she gazed into his eyes. "Yes, brave. Not because of the physical dangers you've faced, and there have been many, but because you've dared to reach out for love. From your son. From me."

He caught her hand and tried to draw her closer.

She backed away and gently disengaged her hand from his. "Not yet."

"I can tell you this much about your secret remedy. I'm not getting any cooler watching you move around in that silk number."

She laughed softly. "Actually, you won't get cooler. The secret is that soon, you'll no longer mind the heat."

"I want you, Leigh."

"I want you, too." She reached for the massage oil. "But there are levels of wanting, levels of pleasure we have yet to explore." She poured a circle of oil in the palm of her hand. It pooled there, warm and moist as the delicate scent of safflower and coconut drifted around her. "Now roll over," she whispered. "And let me worship you."

He held her gaze for a moment, and then he complied. Kneeling beside him, she smoothed the oil over the broad expanse of his muscled back. She anointed several puckered ridges where a bullet or a knife had gouged his flesh, and the violence that had caused the scars flooded into her hands. She took it in, breathing deeply to cleanse herself, and him.

She knew healing physical injuries was possible with her touch, yet now she sought to heal the deeper scars, the ones that didn't show. He moaned as she rotated her palms down his spine, over his firm buttocks. Replenishing her supply of oil, she manipulated the muscles in his thighs and calves. When she reached his feet, she used her thumbs to stimulate, as well as soothe. His breathing quickened.

With long, languorous strokes she returned to his hips, his buttocks, the small of his back, until he grew as pliable as warm clay beneath her fingers, until his breathing synchronized with hers. "Melt for me," she murmured.

Arms flung to the sides, he closed his eyes and surrendered to her rhythm. A slow, steady beat grew through the music, through her kneading fingers. "Give way," she crooned, wanting nothing less than capitulation.

He sighed, a sound wrenched from the depths of his soul.

"Yes." With gentle hands she guided him to his back. He moved with fluid grace born of total relaxation, his eyes closed, lines of care erased from his forehead. She covered his chest with smooth strokes, working the oil into his body, the peace into his soul. And the paradox that she had dreamed of came true. The more he relaxed, the more he surged with desire. His shaft thickened and pulsed. She saved the final massage until last.

Then, when his body obeyed her every pressure, moved in tune with each kneading motion, she swept up that rising expression of his need with one firm stroke, and he groaned the groan of a man carefully, completely aroused.

"I think," she whispered, "that you are ready." Her own preparation had been in tandem with his. Learning his body, she'd schooled her own in the perfect way to fit, to mold, to caress.

Sheathing him became part of the massage as she unrolled the condom slowly, deftly, giving pleasure as she prepared him for greater joy. At last she unclasped the silk toga and allowed it to fall away.

"Open your eyes."

As his lids lifted, the blaze of passion there took her breath away. She had imagined what she was building, but her imagination had failed to conjure up the burning depths in his eyes.

As she rose over him, he grasped her shoulders, his fingers biting into her with a force that stopped just short of pain. His voice was rich with husky desire. "If you've ever loved another man this way..." He paused, holding her tight. "I just might have to kill him."

"No." She drowned in the molten lava of his gaze as she lowered herself, taking him in. "Never another... like this."

He gasped and closed his eyes. "Please," he whispered. "Please."

That he could beg, this man so used to command, was all that she needed to know. Using the rhythm of the ages, she loved him. Desire took him over the edge, pummeling his defenseless body, conquering his will until he arched and cried her name. Over and over. And then, as she melted with him, she called his name, as well, wanting the universe to hear their names spoken together. Then she flew with him across an unbounded and uncharted frontier, a sensuous landscape that would demand no less than all they had to give—forever.

JOE HAD TROUBLE returning to reality—or what he'd always considered to be reality. The mystic world that Leigh offered him when they made love was so powerful that he had to acknowledge its existence, too. How the guys in the precinct would laugh if they saw him now, stretched beneath a woman who believed in crystals, dream-catchers and unicorns. But more important than all of that, she believed in him.

He stroked her shoulder and she stirred, as if coming out of a trance. He'd felt exactly the same way as he'd gradually become aware of birds chirping outside the window and footsteps in the hallway. "Someone may come looking for us soon," he murmured.

"That's likely." She lifted her head and gazed down at him, her hair tumbling around her face and swinging down to tickle his nose.

He ran his fingers through it. "I love your hair."

"I love your mustache." She traced his upper lip.

"I love your eyes." He recognized that they were circling a sensitive topic, playing it safe instead of saying the words they were probably both thinking. But that was okay, for now. They both had a lot to deal with in getting used to such forceful emotions. "I think you've hypnotized me."

She smiled. "A little, perhaps."

"A lot, perhaps."

"I love your eyes, too," she said. "When I first saw you, I thought you looked exactly like a lawman from the streets of Dodge City or Tombstone. I think the right term is *flinty-eyed*."

"You liked that?"

"Sure." She traced the line of his eyebrows. "It showed strength."

"And then I became putty in your hands."

Her smile broadened. "Exactly."

He glanced around the room. "The minute I stepped in the door, I figured out this was your show. What kind of incense is that?"

"Jasmine. For luck . . . and love."

He looked into her eyes and allowed her to see a depth of emotion that he felt unable to voice. "I like it. The music's nice, too."

"And the massage?"

He laughed. "Not bad." His laughter faded and he touched her cheek. "I'm not good at superlatives, but you were . . . amazing."

"I want you to know something. I've never brought another man here. To do so seemed too personal."

A primitive satisfaction flooded through him. "I'm honored."

"Yes, you are. And now we really need to see if Freddy's back." She kissed him lightly and moved away.

He fought the urge to pull her into his arms and say the hell with everybody else. Instead, he caught her hand and caressed her wrist with his thumb. "I'm afraid you've turned me into an addict. Do you think we can manage this disappearing trick again soon?"

Her brown eyes twinkled. "In case you haven't noticed, most people go to bed early around here. And my room is right by the back door. I believe, as one of the owners, you have keys to every door on the ranch."

"That I do." Just the prospect of loving her again in this room tonight was enough to bring a response from his eager body. "But right now I think a cold shower is in order."

"Through there."

Her bathroom was stuffed with aromatic lotions and scented soaps. He scrubbed himself with a loofah and experimented with the pulsing jets on her shower. Such unabashed sensuality really turned him on. He might become a New Age enthusiast yet.

While he dressed and she took her turn in the shower, the scent of the soap she used and the rhythmic pounding of the shower jets affected him so much, he had trouble zipping his jeans. She came out of the shower wrapped in a huge fluffy towel. Ignoring her was not an option.

He drew her into his arms, towel and all, and inhaled her sweet fragrance. "You're delicious," he said, savoring the come-hither look in her eyes. "That's the only word to describe you. You're not a woman, you're an entire life experience."

"Most women are, if given half a chance," she said.

"I plan to give you a whole chance, and then some." He nestled her against his chest and stroked her hair. "Look, I want you to know something, too. Just like you've never brought another man in here, I've never said this to another human being." He hesitated, searching for the right words. "Anything you do, or have done, is okay with me. I'm not sitting in judgment. I just want you to know that."

She stiffened. "I'm not sure what you mean."

He tried again. "I respect your reasons for any actions you've taken, and I want to help. I'll do anything to protect you. So you don't have to be afraid to tell me anything."

She pulled away from him and clutched the towel around her. "You're talking about the sabotage, aren't you?"

"Yes."

"And you still think I know something I'm not telling you?"

"Leigh, it's logical that you're involved. You have the strongest motive. What I'm trying to say is that I understand. I'm sure it got out of control and now you don't know where to turn. Turn to me. I want to help you."

Her eyes became dark pools of fury. "Do you imagine I could love you like that—" she swung an arm at the bed "—and still be holding a terrible secret from you?" She began to shake. "That sort of loving means stripping away *everything* false. You can't have that kind of experience if you're keeping things from each other!"

"But—"

"I have made a mistake." Her eyes filled with pain. "I wanted you so much that I imagined you were ready for what I have to give. Obviously you're not."

His mind whirled, trying to grasp that she was rejecting him. No. She couldn't be slamming the door of paradise in his face. It wasn't possible.

"Go."

"Don't do this," he murmured. "I'm only trying to tell you that I—"

"Think I'm a liar?" She lifted her chin with such regal poise that he imagined a goddess preparing to smite some poor mortal with a thunderbolt for his audacity. "As long as you can think that, we have no reason to breathe the same air. Now go."

*Breathe the same air.* Ah, she had such a way of phrasing things. That was exactly what he wanted to do, for the rest of his life. But he'd poisoned the air between them with his suspicion. He could not take it back. She was right, he did have doubts. By her standards, doubts were not allowed. There was no arguing with that.

He picked up his hat from a chair and settled it on his head. Then he touched the brim. "Ma'am." He didn't look back as he walked out the door.

# 15

THE FLURRY OF ACTIVITIES in the days preceding the rodeo kept Leigh busy enough for her to submerge her sense of betrayal. She tried to take comfort in the growing intimacy between Kyle and his father. Joe had made progress, astounding progress, really. She'd expected too much from a man used to suspecting the worst from everyone. She assumed that eventually he'd solve the mystery of the accidents around the ranch. When he did, she'd be vindicated, but that would be too late. Joe would have to believe in her on faith alone, before he uncovered the facts that cleared her name, or all was lost.

Two days before the rodeo, Amanda, Chase and little Bart returned from New York. Amanda had convinced her advertising agency to open a branch in Tucson, and Amanda's family had been delighted to meet Chase. Leigh was thrilled for Chase, who had become as close to her as a brother in the months he'd lived at the True Love.

No sooner had Chase and Amanda unpacked than they asked Belinda to watch the baby so they could take a horseback ride with Leigh.

"Are you sure you want me to go?" Leigh asked as they all saddled up. "I can understand wanting to get on a horse again after all that time back East, but you two probably haven't had much time alone since you left."

"Yes, we want you along," Chase said firmly. "We want to go up and see how the reconstruction's coming on the pond, for one thing, and with the hands up there building the dam, we wouldn't have much privacy, anyway. Besides, we have a few things to tell you."

Leigh was secretly glad for any excuse to get away from the ranch for a while. She kept running into Joe, and keeping up a pleasant exterior was becoming increasingly difficult.

On the way up the canyon, Amanda and Chase exclaimed over the damage caused by the flash flood.

"I was hoping Joe would have solved this business by the time we got back," Chase said. "Doesn't he have any idea who's behind the accidents?"

Leigh decided not to mention that she was Joe's chief suspect. "It's difficult working on his own and trying to keep the investigation quiet. When the dam was dynamited, he and Ry talked about putting in an insurance claim, but the insurance company would have sent investigators out here."

Chase sighed. "If Joe doesn't solve this soon, we'll have to call in the police. We've been lucky nobody's been seriously hurt. Or killed."

Leigh shivered. Joe thought she had something to do with incidents that could have cost lives. The concept made her soul ache with the injustice of it.

She, Chase and Amanda inspected the progress on the pond. A temporary dam had been constructed farther upstream, and now the hands were replacing the rocks at the original dam site. All the dead fish had been hauled away, but the scummy bottom of the pond still didn't smell very appetizing.

"Yuck," Amanda said, wrinkling her nose. "Let's go upstream." She turned her horse and started up the canyon.

A muscle in Chase's jaw twitched as he eyed the scene. "I would love to get my hands on the jerk that did this. In fact, I look forward to meeting him. He has a lot to answer for."

"Don't forget that Duane and Belinda are still on Joe's list of suspects."

Chase shook his head. "Neither of them was responsible for this."

"Try telling Joe that." Leigh realized she'd revealed some of her bitterness when Chase glanced at her, a question in his green eyes. She waved a hand dismissively. "Don't mind me. We've had an eventful few days while you've been gone."

"I take it you and Gilardini aren't getting along?"

"You could say that."

"Do you want to tell me about it?"

She gave him a weary smile. "Maybe. But not right now. I agree with Amanda. Let's go upstream."

They found a spot near the temporary dam where a gnarled oak provided enough shade for all three of them. They dismounted, tethered the horses and carried their canteens under the tree.

"Okay," Leigh said when everyone was settled. "What's the big news?"

"We didn't want to make a general announcement, but we wanted you to know," Amanda said. "We found out about Chase's mother."

Leigh's gaze swung to Chase and he nodded, a sad smile playing over his face. Raised in a series of foster homes with no idea who his father was and no knowledge of his mother's whereabouts, he'd been ashamed of his background for most of his adult life. Amanda had encouraged him to confront his past and try to find his mother. "You don't look very happy about what you found," Leigh said.

"It's not a happy story, but I'm glad I know it." He reached for Amanda's hand. "If Amanda hadn't come into my life, I'd have gone on believing my mother wasn't a very nice person."

"You're speaking in the past tense," Leigh said.

"Yeah." Chase sighed. "We found out where she's buried, in a grungy little cemetery. We're buying her a decent headstone. Amanda helped me with the words on it. *Helen Marie Lavette, mother of Chase. She gave everything she had.*" Chase looked up, his eyes bright, his voice husky. "And she did."

As if sensing Chase would have difficulty telling the story, Amanda took up the tale. Through a medallion Chase wore that had belonged to his mother, they'd located Helen's grammar school and eventually one of her old classmates, Suzanne, who'd kept in touch with her. They learned that Helen had been managing to support her only child with a series of minimum-wage jobs, but she had no family, no safety net of any kind. Then she developed cancer and knew she would waste away, possibly traumatizing her small son. She'd put him in foster care before the deterioration started. As long as she had the strength, she'd kept tabs on him, creeping up to the window of the house where he lived or peering over the fence to watch him playing in the yard, until she was hospitalized for the last weeks of her life.

"She must have loved you very much," Leigh said, her throat tight.

Chase swallowed and stared at the toe of his boot. "Yep."

"We're keeping our fingers crossed that our next baby will be a girl," Amanda said, "so we can name her Helen Marie."

Leigh focused on them and allowed her mind to expand beyond this moment under an oak tree. "I think you will have a little girl," she said with a smile.

Chase looked at her. "You think or you know?"

Leigh chuckled. "Actually, I know, but I usually pretend I'm not sure, so people won't freak out."

"We won't freak out," Chase said with a grin. "We know you're weird, and we love you for it." He got to his feet and helped Amanda up. "We'd better get back. We're not keeping the story about my mother a secret, exactly. We just wanted you to be the first to know." He glanced at her. "Unless you knew all this already?"

"No, I didn't." Leigh got up and brushed off the seat of her jeans. "If I had, I would have told you and saved you a heck of a lot of trouble. I don't have unlimited pyschic power. If I did, I'd have figured out who's causing the accidents." Not that Joe would believe her if she did, she thought. Then, for some reason, she remembered the diary page that she'd pulled from the cactus. "You must have had to plow through some old records to find your mother," she said to Chase.

"Amanda did. She's a whiz at that."

Leigh glanced at her. "Joe has something we found out in the desert that looks like a photocopy of an old diary page. If you'd be willing to take it down to the Arizona Historical Society, we might find out what diary it came from. I told Joe I didn't think it was important, but it keeps flashing into my mind. That means there's something to it."

"Consider it done," Amanda said. "I'm hopelessly inadequate at helping build a rodeo arena, so this will make me feel useful."

THE NIGHT BEFORE the rodeo, just before sunset, Joe went with everyone else to admire the new arena and welcome the delivery of Grateful Dead, Eb Whitlock's Brahma bull. Chase, Amanda and little Bart rode the half mile to the arena with Leigh in her pickup. Ry and Freddy took Kyle with them, and Joe rode in the back.

Ever since the afternoon he and Leigh had made love, Joe had prayed for a cleansing vision that would convince him Leigh had nothing to do with the sabotage. Unfortunately, he'd been cursed with a logical mind that preferred careful deductions to cleansing visions. He was ninety-nine percent sure she was telling the truth, but he couldn't say that to her and expect anything but disdain. He had to come to her free of doubt, and he knew it.

The entrance to the arena parking area was on the main road leading to the highway. An arch over the gate announced the True Love Rodeo Grounds, bracketed on either side by a heart with an arrow through it. Ry tooted his horn as he led the way under the arch. An afternoon rain had washed down the arena and the tang of wet creosote bushes mingled with the fragrance of new lumber. Ry had floated a loan to construct the modest structure, which included several holding pens, bleachers, two bucking chutes and a small judges' stand.

While Ry stood by proudly, everyone exclaimed over the finished arena and speculated as to how much revenue it could bring in during the year. But a cloud of dust on the entrance road ended the discussion as all eyes focused on the arrival of Grateful Dead.

"Your nemesis is on his way," Freddy said to Ry.

"The man or the animal?" Ry asked. "I have far more reservations about Whitlock than I do about his bull."

"I found out where that diary page came from," Amanda said as the shiny dual-wheeled pickup came into sight. "The guy who wrote it was named Whitlock, too. Jethro Whitlock."

"Maybe he's related," Kyle said.

"That's probably why the diary page was out there," Joe said. It looked like another dead end. He watched as Eb parked the truck and climbed out. "Some amateur historian found the diary at the historical society and is trying to prove a link between that Whitlock and the one who owns the Rocking W Ranch."

"I'm going to start reading it tonight," Amanda said to Joe. "I'll let you know if anything turns up."

"Can I read it after you?" Kyle asked.

"Sure." Amanda squeezed his shoulder. "But it won't be as sweet as Clara's diary, I'm afraid. This guy sounds like a rough character. Went around robbing banks and stage lines until he was finally caught and thrown into the Yuma Territorial Prison. I guess he died there, which was probably a relief to the citizens of Arizona."

Eb parked the truck with a flourish and climbed out. "Well, I brought your star attraction," he boomed. "How do you like my trailer? You could leave it parked out front to get people's attention."

"Looks big enough for a circus elephant," Ry said, glancing at the large purple trailer with Grateful Dead, The Bull That's Never Been Rode stenciled on the side in gold.

Eb hitched up his belt. "That's so my boys can cross-tie him in the middle and he won't be able to throw himself against the sides and get hurt. See that slot along each side? That's my invention. A cowboy can be on either side of the trailer on the outside and move that bull in slick as a whistle. Had to come up with something. None of my hands would walk into the trailer with him." Eb glanced at the group. "In any case, I'd advise taking the little ones to one of your trucks before we bring him out, just to be on the safe side."

Freddy glanced at Ry. "Isn't it nice to know you're planning to ride an animal like that?" She turned to Amanda, who was holding Bart and looking alarmed. "Let's go, Amanda. Kyle, why don't you come with us into my truck? We'll turn on the radio and sing some songs while these macho guys show how tough they are."

Kyle glanced at Joe and Joe nodded. "Good idea, buddy. This bull is no Romeo, from what I hear."

"Are you staying, Dad?"

"Yes."

Kyle squared his shoulders. "Then so am I."

Joe felt caught in a trap of his own making. He loved the courage that Kyle demonstrated; the little guy had come a long way since the day they'd arrived at the True Love. If Joe ordered him into the truck, Kyle might feel put down, yet this bull made Joe nervous. He glanced at Leigh, seeking some signal, some silent communication that would help him decide what to do. For the first time he could remember since he'd met her, she gave no indication of what she was thinking. She seemed to have withdrawn into herself.

"Just keep the boy out of the way, then," Eb said. "I brought the cattle prod to use on him."

Leigh roused herself. "Don't use the cattle prod."

Eb paused and looked at her as if she'd come unhinged. "What do you mean, don't use it? This animal is hard to control, Leigh. You've seen him."

"Let me talk to him."

"Let you—" Eb stared at her.

"I want everybody away from that trailer," Leigh said. "He hates it when people crowd around."

Ry stepped toward her. "Leigh, you know how much faith I have in you, but this bull is legendary. Let's not take any foolish chances."

She faced him, her expression composed. "The foolishness would be for all of you to converge on him and jolt him out of the trailer with a cattle prod. I can guarantee somebody will get hurt if you do that. Now, I'm going over to the trailer to talk with him." She started across the parking lot. "I'm warning you to stay back," she called over her shoulder.

"Leigh—"

"Let her do it, Ry." Joe was surprised to hear himself say it. He didn't want Leigh to put herself in danger. Why was he so certain that she would be okay? Logically she had no business dealing with a two-thousand-pound Brahma bull.

"Yeah," Kyle echoed. "Let her."

Ry glanced at Chase, who shrugged. "Doesn't seem like a problem if she talks to him," Chase said. "He's still in the trailer. He can't do anything from there."

"No, it's a strong trailer." Eb shook his head. "But you boys humor Leigh far too much with this voodoo hocus-pocus of hers. If you want her to sweet-talk Grateful Dead, be my guest, but it won't accomplish anything."

As Joe watched Leigh move to the front of the trailer and look in through the metal grille, he could swear she seemed to be standing in a pool of light. He glanced at the setting sun, sure it was a trick of the clouds rimming the horizon, but he couldn't figure out the trajectories that would bring a beam of sunlight to fall directly on Leigh.

She stayed at the head of the trailer for several minutes while the men waited in tense silence. Then she walked to the back. Before Joe realized what she was doing, she had the tailgate unlatched.

"Hey!" Ry called, starting over at a run. Joe followed.

Leigh spun and held up a hand. "Stop right there."

Ry skidded to a halt and Joe nearly bumped into him. He felt a body thump into his and turned to see Chase over his right shoulder.

A smile twitched at the corner's of Leigh's mouth. "Will you guys ease up before you hurt yourselves? I can handle this."

Grateful Dead kicked the side of the trailer and bawled out a warning.

"You're not going in there," Ry said.

"How else can I lead him out?"

"With the ropes on the sides, like Whitlock said," Chase suggested.

"He'll try to get away once he's out of the trailer if you treat him like that. He's in a strange place, and he's very nervous." She turned away from them as another metallic thump came from inside the trailer. "I'm going in."

"Aw, Leigh," Chase said. "We can't let you do that."

"*Let?*" She whirled and glared at all three of them. "Six months ago, you three greenhorns had never laid eyes on a steer, let alone a Brahma bull."

"*Greenhorns?*" they chorused.

"Don't think you can tell me how to handle this animal. I have more experience than the three of you put together, with Eb Whitlock thrown in for good measure!"

Ry braced his hands on his hips. "And here I thought you were the reasonable sister. You've got more of Freddy in you than I thought."

"The fact is, we both have a lot of Clara in us. Now back off, all of you."

"No, by God," Ry said, starting forward. "I—"

Joe caught his arm. "She can do it."

Ry turned to stare at Joe. "How the hell do you know? You're the greenest one of the bunch!"

"That's true, but I know Leigh." He felt as if the words were flowing through him, not from him. "If she says she can handle that bull, I believe her."

Ry took off his hat and scratched his head. Then he peered at Joe as if his partner had taken leave of his senses. Yet Joe had never felt more alive, more joyous in his life. He couldn't have explained the exact connection between Leigh's fearless handling of the bull and her truthfulness about the accidents, but there was one. It wasn't logical, but it was real.

Ry put his hat on and tugged it over his eyes. "I don't like this. If anything happens to that woman, I'm holding you responsible, Gilardini."

"All right." Joe gazed across at Leigh. Now, when she looked at him, the mask was gone, and her spirit shone forth so brightly he caught his breath. "I'll take the responsibility," he said.

"Chase, go get a couple of ropes to have ready," Ry said. "Just in case Grateful Dead isn't a true believer in the power of psychic connections."

"What's Leigh gonna do, Dad?"

Joe glanced down to see Kyle standing next to him. If Grateful Dead bolted from the trailer, Kyle would be much too close for comfort. But the bull wouldn't bolt. Confidence in Leigh overrode Joe's fear. "She's going to talk that bull out of the trailer, Kyle. She's connecting with his mind, just the way she does with horses."

"And people," Kyle said.

"Yes, and people." He believed, yet he held his breath as Leigh edged into the trailer, crooning to the bull with every step. When another thump of hooves against metal interrupted her litany, Joe winced.

"I thought you had complete faith in this project," Ry said, eyeing him.

Joe kept his gaze on the trailer. "I do."

"They say love is blind," Ry said.

Joe didn't respond. He'd never been able to see more clearly in his life, but it was a different sort of seeing, and he wasn't about to explain it to Ry right now.

"Here they come," Kyle whispered.

Joe clenched his jaw as Leigh emerged, holding the halter of the ugliest animal he'd ever seen. Horns curved viciously forward above a white death-mask face with dark splotches around each eye. The menacing hump above his massive brindle shoulders swayed as he walked. Next to him, Leigh looked no bigger than a child. Joe had witnessed some unbelievable acts of courage during his twenty years as a cop, but he'd never seen anything more heart-stopping than the picture of this slight young woman leading a beast that could crush her in an instant if it chose to do so.

Leigh didn't break her concentration as she moved slowly down the ramp, her head close to the bull's ear while she kept up a constant flow of soothing words. She walked away from the trailer toward the sturdy pen designated for the bull, and Joe followed her with his eyes, his heart full. Careful to keep her movements steady, she unlatched the gate and led the bull inside. When she latched the gate after her, closing herself inside with the animal, Joe thought he might pass out.

She stood there for long moments scratching the monster's nose. Then she unhooked the lead rope and turned her back on the bull as she unlatched the gate again and walked out. An audible sigh went up from the group watching her.

Joe didn't consciously decide to go to meet her, yet suddenly he was on his way, eating up the space that separated them with long strides. When they were face-to-face, she stared up at him.

"I believe you," he said.

"I know you do." Her bottomless gaze drew him in and her mysterious smile made him tremble with anticipation.

"Leigh, I—"

"Hey, that was some trick!" called Whitlock.

Joe turned to see him barreling over, destroying any chance for Joe to say what was burning in his heart. His buddies knew enough to hang back when they'd figured out what was happening, but not this blowhard. Where was Chase with a rope when a guy needed one?

"I wouldn't have believed it if I hadn't seen it with my own eyes," Eb said as he reached them.

Joe glanced over to where Ry, Chase and Kyle stood. All of them, including Kyle, looked highly amused. Joe wasn't.

Whitlock compounded his boorish behavior by clapping Joe on the back. "You guys sure have been hanging in there with this ranch. I'm surprised, to tell the truth. Thought you'd have given up and cleared out by now, especially with all the things going wrong recently."

Joe gazed down at Leigh. "I'd say everything's going along pretty well right now."

"I suppose you still think you'll make a big profit when you sell to the developers in a couple of years, but with interest rates going up, I wouldn't count on that," Whitlock said. "We could be in for another real-estate slump. Frankly, I think you'd be better off to sell now."

Joe had trouble wrenching his attention away from Leigh, but something in Whitlock's tone niggled at him. He forced himself to look into the guy's eyes. Was it his imagination, or was there a spark of desperation behind the genial smile, the hearty advice? He decided to probe a little deeper. "There's a good chance we won't ever sell the True Love," he said.

Whitlock's smile stayed in place but his eyes narrowed. "That's crazy. You're just city boys playing at running a ranch."

"I wouldn't bet on it." Joe met the challenge in Whitlock's eyes.

Whitlock's smile faded and he looked away, his glance darting everywhere but at Joe. "You'll never succeed. Haven't you heard? The True Love is cursed."

*I've got you, you son of a bitch. Now I just have to find proof.* Joe stepped over beside Leigh and slipped an arm around her waist. "You know, Whitlock, I have the strongest feeling that curse is about to be lifted."

# 16

"IT'S WHITLOCK. I just don't have a way to prove it yet," Joe said later that evening as he sat with Ry, Freddy and Chase on the patio. Kyle was out on the front porch with Dexter, and Amanda was putting Bart to bed. Joe had chosen the patio for the discussion because it was fairly private. The number of guests had swelled in the past week due to the publicity about the rodeo, and most of them were gathered in the main room of the house for line-dancing lessons conducted by Leigh.

Joe could see her rhythmic motions through the large window, and they fired his blood. He longed to ditch the investigation and take her back to her room for a night of lovemaking. But he had a job to do, and the job affected her welfare, too.

"You know I agree with you," Ry said. "I've never trusted him."

Freddy shifted in her lawn chair. "I still can't believe it's Eb. Not when we're talking about a dangerous brushfire and a flash flood that could have killed Leigh and Kyle. Eb wouldn't do things like that just to get a piece of land."

"It's more than the land," Joe said. "And once we find out what he's after, we'll have our proof. What about mineral rights? Could there be oil under here?"

Freddy shook her head. "My dad had geologists come out more than once. There's no oil in the ground, or precious metal in the canyons, either."

"Then it's something else," Joe said. "And we have to come up with it fast. He's liable to create an accident during the rodeo tomorrow. I'm worried about—" Joe paused as Kyle came through the French doors and walked across the patio toward them. "Hi, buddy."

"Belinda says it's time for me to go to bed. The dancing's about over."

"Good idea," Joe said. "Tomorrow's a big day."

Kyle came over and leaned on Joe's chair. "I told Dexter about that Jethro Whitlock guy who wrote the diary Amanda's reading. He got kind of excited."

Freddy laughed. "Dexter hates anybody with the name of Whitlock. He caught Eb giving Belinda a kiss on the cheek once, and he's been jealous ever since."

Joe glanced at Chase. "Is Amanda planning to read the rest of that diary tonight?"

"If she can keep her eyes open." Chase stretched. "We're both still suffering from jet lag."

"I think we all need a good night's rest," Leigh said, coming out to the patio. "I'm beat. You can stay up all night discussing this if you want, but I'm going to bed."

Joe gazed up at her, trying to decide if her announcement was an invitation or a rejection. They'd had no time alone since she'd taken Grateful Dead to his pen, and now she seemed determined to avoid his questioning glance. He stood and turned to his son. "Go get ready for bed, Kyle. I'll come and tuck you in in a minute."

"See you all in the morning," Leigh said, starting toward the back patio gate that would provide a shortcut to her room.

Joe followed her. "Leigh."

She turned just inside the gate. "Yes?"

He lowered his voice, aware they might be overheard by Chase, Ry and Freddy. "We need to talk." *I need to make love to you.*

She laid a hand on his arm. "I can see how involved you are with the investigation, and God knows it needs to be solved, for all our sakes. I'll see you in the morning."

Her rejection knocked the breath out of him. "But—"

"Good night, Joe." She slipped through the gate and was gone, leaving him totally confused. He'd seen the light in her eyes when he'd walked out to meet her at the rodeo grounds. He'd expected clear sailing from that moment on. What the hell had happened?

AN HOUR INTO THE RODEO the next afternoon, Leigh surveyed the crowd from the bed of a open wagon drawn up beside the stands. Belinda and Dexter were sitting next to her on lawn chairs, with Kyle on Dexter's far side, and a vacant chair ready for Amanda and Bart, who were due to arrive at any moment. A canvas awning provided shade. It was Ry's creative suggestion to provide a comfortable spot for Belinda, Dexter, Amanda and the baby. Dexter had requested that Kyle join them. Following her team-roping event with Ry, Leigh had climbed up on the wagon to see if anyone in the group needed anything.

"We're fine," Belinda assured her. "You and Ry were wonderful, by the way. I yelled myself hoarse."

"It was fun." Leigh was proud of the way she and Ry had worked together in their first competition. Pussywillow wasn't as well trained as Penny Lover, but she was adequate. Ry had ridden Red Devil and the big gelding had performed well. They hadn't won the event, but they'd come close.

"Kyle's father certainly has been busy today," Belinda commented.

"He has a lot on his mind," Leigh said. She knew Joe had checked and rechecked every detail of the rodeo to make sure Eb Whitlock hadn't sabotaged anything. He'd kept a constant eye on Eb, who'd spent the day strutting around the rodeo grounds bragging about Grateful Dead's upcoming performance. Leigh had tried to stay out of Joe's way, knowing he was in full cop mode. The strength of her feelings would only interfere with his concentration.

She listened to the rodeo announcer describe the bareback bronc-riding event and searched the area around the bucking chutes, figuring Joe would be down there making sure everything was going smoothly. She couldn't find him. She scanned the crowd and the perimeter of the arena and still couldn't locate him.

The announcer finished his introduction. *"But before we continue the event, I have someone here with something to say to a certain young lady."*

The microphone crackled. *"Leigh, this is Joe. I've been trying to talk to you all day but you keep ducking me."*

Warmth washed over her and she placed a hand over her racing heart. She could feel the attention of everyone in the arena focused on the little wagon beside the stands.

*"I'd order you to meet me, but I know Singleton women don't take kindly to orders. So if you can spare the time, come to Grateful Dead's pen immediately. Please."*

The stands erupted in laughter and Leigh's face flamed. She glanced at Kyle, who was staring at her with his mouth open. Speechless herself, she could only shrug and give him a silly smile.

"I think you'd better go meet him, sweetheart," Belinda said gently, giving her a nudge. "No telling what message he'll put on the P.A. system next."

Leigh stumbled down from the wagon in a daze. Surely she was dreaming. Joe Gilardini, the man who kept his feelings guarded more carefully than Fort Knox, wouldn't announce his relationship with her over a loudspeaker. As she skirted the arena fence, a few cowboys called out kidding remarks, but then the announcer started the bronc-riding event, and everyone's attention returned to the competition.

Everyone's except for the tall cowboy standing next to Grateful Dead's pen. Joe's gaze, steady and sure, drew her closer.

She shook her head. "I can't believe you did that."

"Can't you? I'm a desperate man. You won't have anything to do with me."

"I'm trying to help!"

"By frustrating the daylights out of me?" He took a stride forward and grabbed her elbows. "Just when I have everything figured out, you're nowhere to be found!"

"You've figured out why Whitlock wants this place?"

"No, you crazy idiot." He smiled gently. "I've figured out that I'm hopelessly in love with you."

She stared up at him in total shock. Of all the ways she'd imagined he'd finally break down and tell her, declaring it in the middle of a crowded rodeo grounds while he was working on the sabotage case was not one of them.

"Well, don't you have anything to say?" he demanded.

"You're at the climax of an investigation!"

His gray eyes danced. "But that's not the climax I keep thinking about."

Desire blossomed in her, but she fought her reaction. "You have to concentrate and forget about me for now," she said with as much firmness as she could muster.

He pulled her close. "I can't."

She tried to put some space between them, but he wouldn't allow it. "Now, Joe, I'm sure that after twenty years you've learned how to block out your emotions at a time like this."

"So I did." He looked down at her, his gaze smoldering. "But you've changed me. I can't block you out. I want to hold you, to make love to you."

She felt momentary panic. What had she done?

"Don't look so scared," he said gently. "I'm still a good cop. I'll figure this guy out. But I can't go it alone anymore. Even if we can't make love this minute, I need to know that we will, and soon. Most of all, I have to know that you're on my side."

She cupped his face in both hands, and her eyes filled with tears. "Oh, yes. A thousand times, yes! I was saving this moment for when we could concentrate completely on each other. I didn't realize..."

"That I needed you?"

"Forgive me, my darling." She blocked out the noisy crowd and the flurry of activity around them. She blocked out everything except the passion in his gray eyes. "I love you, Joe," she said, tears of happiness rolling down her cheeks. "You're the missing part of me, the man I've been searching for all my life."

"And I was such a fool, I didn't know I was searching. But I was." He lowered his mouth to hers. "And I found you," he whispered just before he claimed her lips.

"Joe!"

With a muttered oath, he lifted his head.

"I'm sorry, Joe. Leigh." Chase paused to catch his breath. "But Amanda's found something in that diary. Jethro Whitlock knew Clara Singleton. He mentioned her several times and said something in the diary about going back after what was his. It could have been Clara, but it also could have been a shipment of gold he took from the Butterfield Stage. The gold from that robbery was never recovered, and it would be worth several million now. Amanda thinks it's buried on the ranch."

Joe released Leigh and turned to Chase. "Would Whitlock know about the diary?"

"Just before we came down here we called the Arizona Historical Society. They remembered Whitlock coming in there during the past year, and apparently he was interested in the diary."

"Then we'd better have a little talk with Whitlock."

"That's just it," Chase said. "He's disappeared. Ry's supposed to ride Grateful Dead in about fifteen minutes, so you'd think he'd be around for that."

"Unless he's gone after the gold now, knowing half the valley would be watching his bull pulverize Ry," Joe said.

"There's another thing," Chase added. "Kyle just interpreted this from something Dexter was trying to say over at the wagon. Dexter seems to think the gold could be buried under the old homestead floor."

Joe looked at Leigh. "That's it," he said. "Everything falls into place now. Leigh and I scared off a couple of guys out there the other night. They must have been sent out to start digging."

Chase's eyes narrowed. "And now, while everybody's at the rodeo—"

"Let's go," Joe said. "We'll be less conspicuous on horseback than if we take one of the trucks."

"I'll ride Destiny," Chase said, loping off toward the pens where the cutting horses were kept.

"Take Pussywillow, Joe," Leigh said. "She's fast."

"Good idea." He started off toward the pens just as Ry rode up on Red Devil.

He wheeled his horse in front of Joe. "Amanda just told me the story."

"We think Whitlock's at the homestead. Lavette and I are riding out there."

Ry tugged his hat over his eyes. "So am I."

"You have an event in less than fifteen minutes," Joe reminded him.

Ry grinned. "Maybe I won't have to ride that bull, after all." He held out a hand to Joe. "Hop on. I'll give you a lift to the holding pens."

Joe started to get on without a backward glance. Leigh wondered if he'd forgotten she was standing there. Then he seemed to catch himself and came back to her.

He gripped her arms and his gaze was intent. "Take care of Kyle for me."

She gasped. "Don't say things like that. You're coming back."

He smiled at her. "Of course I am. I meant just for the next hour or so. I don't want him to worry about what we're up to."

"I'll take care of him." She concentrated hard, surrounding Joe with protective light.

"I love you," he murmured. Then he vaulted to the back of Ry's horse and they galloped away.

Leigh knew that if she kept very quiet and focused on what was about to happen out at the homestead, she would know how the coming confrontation would turn out. If millions of dollars was at stake, Eb would be a dangerous enemy. By using her powers, she could find out whether Joe would emerge unscathed . . . or not. She wiped all thought of the homestead from her mind as she hurried over to the wagon to reassure Kyle.

JOE, Ry and Chase cut across a little-used trail to reach the riverbed, then doubled back toward the homestead, approaching at a slow walk with Joe in the lead. He paused and held up his hand to call a halt. As he listened, sorting through the rustling of animals in the brush and the chirping of birds, he heard the rhythmic sounds of shovels biting into the dirt. Joe reached into his boot and pulled out his .38.

He nudged Pussywillow and motioned the other two men to follow him. He had the only gun, but Ry and Chase had ropes and knew how to use them far better than he did. Joe was counting on the element of surprise to give them an advantage, as well as something less tangible. Whitlock was after money. Joe and his partners cared about something more important than that. They were fighting for their home.

Closer in, he heard voices and held up his hand again. Turning in his saddle, he used gestures and mouthed instructions to send Chase around to his left, Ry around to his right. He'd explained on the way over that he would go in first, gun drawn. If Whitlock and his men offered no resistance, Chase and Ry could ride in afterward and help tie them up. If they did offer resistance, then Joe hoped his partners were as good at roping two-legged critters as they seemed to be with four-legged ones.

Joe started forward again. Through the mesquite branches he could see them—two men besides Whitlock. A battered old truck with a winch on the front bumper was pulled up close to the hole they'd made in the floor of the homestead, and they were straining to get two cables fastened around something in the hole. If they hadn't been totally engrossed in hauling a fortune out of the ground, they would have heard him approach. But buried treasure had made them temporarily deaf.

Whitlock was the only one armed. He had a handgun in a holster on his hip. He stood back and allowed his men to do the dirty work. Joe decided to let them get the gold all the way out before he interrupted their little party. Ingots were damned heavy.

Cursing and sweating, the men positioned the cables beneath the chest and tightened them. The winch whined as one man operated it and the other steadied the rusty black strongbox coming out of the hole. Finally, they had it out, and Whitlock hurried over to throw open the lid. All three men gasped.

So did Joe. The chest was stacked tight with gold bars. Even tarnished a rusty brown with age, they gleamed with promise. Whitlock reached out a hand, and Joe called out.

"Get 'em up, all of you!"

They whirled in his direction, but only one of Whitlock's men lifted his hands in the air. The other grabbed for a shovel, and Joe shot it out of his hand. The man howled and held his bleeding wrist against his stomach.

The distraction gave Whitlock time to draw his gun and get off a shot. Joe's right forearm burned as the bullet passed through, nicking the same bone he'd broken in the elevator. The force of the bullet flung his gun from his hand. As Whitlock raised his gun for a second shot, a rope sailed over his shoulders and snapped tight, throwing him to the ground. The gun discharged into the air as he landed.

Ry leapt from Red Devil's saddle as the big horse sat back on his haunches, keeping the rope taut around

Whitlock. The uninjured man grabbed a sledgehammer. Swinging it over his head, he started for Ry. He never made it. Chase's loop caught him around the ankle, jerking his leg out from under him.

Joe dismounted and ran over to grab Whitlock's gun in his left hand, but as he did, the injured man fled into the brush.

"Destiny and I will get him," Chase said. While Ry covered the guy on the ground, Chase loosened his rope and flicked it from the man's ankle. Then he coiled it and headed into the brush after his quarry.

Joe held the gun while Ry, using his best calf-tying techniques, trussed up Whitlock and his hired hand.

"How'd you know?" Whitlock cried, his face contorted with fury. "How the hell did you guys know?"

Joe gazed at him. "We got the word from Clara."

"Come on." Whitlock spat in the dirt. "You don't believe that claptrap any more than I do." He glared at his hired hand. "One of you guys talked, didn't you?"

"No, but they got a little careless," Joe said.

When Ry finished tying both men securely, he turned to Joe. "You're bleeding pretty bad."

"A pressure bandage ought to do it." Joe glanced down at Whitlock, who was still dressed in the showy Western shirt he'd worn to the rodeo. "Why don't you tear up Whitlock's shirt?"

"It would be a pleasure."

"That's a fifty-dollar shirt!" Whitlock bellowed.

"Where you're going, they provide free clothes." Joe sat down and trained the gun on Whitlock while Ry ripped off the front of his shirt, created a makeshift bandage and bound it to Joe's arm with strips from the same shirt.

"Same ol', same ol'," Joe said as Ry worked on the bandage. "You realize this is the same damned arm I broke in the elevator. I get hurt every time I'm around you, McGuinnes."

"Yeah, but just like I told you in the elevator, Gilardini, I'm also going to make you rich." Ry tied the last knot and stood just as Chase came trotting in, his prisoner at the end of his lariat.

"Hog-tie him, Ry," Chase said, dismounting and coming over to Joe. "How's the arm?"

"I'll make it."

Ry finished trussing up the last prisoner and ambled over to stand next to Chase. He pushed back his hat. "Damn, but that was fun."

Chase grinned. "Can't remember when I've had a better time with my clothes on."

Joe studied his two partners. "For a couple of civilians, you were passable."

"Passable?" Ry cried. "We were great! The three of us make a hell of a team."

Joe chuckled. "Too bad you have such a small ego, McGuinnes."

Ry turned to Chase. "Weren't we great?"

"I'll tell you who was great. Destiny. I'm riding that horse from now on. He can *move*."

"Give Red Devil another year and he'll be almost that good. Give him five years and he'll—"

"You're not talking much like a guy who plans to turn a profit by selling the place," Joe observed.

Ry and Chase stared at him.

"Wasn't that the idea?" Joe tried to keep a straight face as his two partners grew more and more uncomfortable. "Aw, hell," Joe said finally, breaking into a smile. "I don't want to sell, either. You were right, Ry. The place grows on you."

"I heard that," cried Leigh, reining in Mikey and leaping to the ground. "You have a witness." She ran over to Joe and dropped to her knees beside him. "I would think a man of your experience could avoid getting shot," she said, her voice husky as she examined the makeshift bandage. "Did it go all the way through?"

"Yes, ma'am." He drank in the sight of her. Maybe it was the loss of blood affecting his vision, but he could swear she was surrounded by that darned halo of light again. "I was lucky."

"Lucky? You got shot!"

"Any bullet that doesn't kill you is a lucky bullet," he said. "The way I figure it, someone was watching over me."

She gazed into his eyes and swallowed hard. "Someone was."

"Hey, why are you here, anyway?" Joe asked, remembering his last instructions to her. "I thought I told you to stay and take care of Kyle."

Freddy rode up and dismounted. "You have a short memory, Joe. Just recently, you announced to the world that Singleton women don't take kindly to orders." She unstrapped her first-aid kit from her saddle.

"Where *is* Kyle?" Joe asked.

"With Dexter," Leigh said, stepping back so Freddy could look at Joe's wound. She waited anxiously while Freddy checked Joe's vital signs and examined the bandage. "How bad is it?"

"Not too bad. The bleeding's about stopped. You're a lucky guy."

"Absolutely," Joe said, gazing up at Leigh.

"Wouldn't you just know it? Now here comes Amanda!" Chase cried in an exasperated tone. "After I specifically told her to stay with Bart. Pardon my French, honey bun, but what the hell are you doing out here? And where's our son?"

Amanda swung down from the saddle and tied her horse to a tree. "Our son is with Belinda," she said, striding toward him. "Freddy, Leigh and I had a little talk and decided we had as much right to be out here fighting for the True Love as any of you. Then on the way we heard shots and put on the speed. Leigh outran us. How is he, Freddy?"

"He'll be fine."

"Thank God." Amanda glanced at the rusted chest and did a double take. "Is that *real?*"

Ry turned to Whitlock. "Tell her, neighbor." Whitlock just glared at him. "Aw, he must not be feeling too neighborly," Ry said. "To answer your question, Amanda, I believe you're looking at the gold shipment from the Butterfield Stage robbery pulled off by Jethro Whitlock about a hundred and ten years ago."

Amanda walked over to the chest. "Wow." She gazed down at the gold bars. "Did you notice there's a piece of paper tucked in here?"

"Probably some invoice," Ry said. "But we might as well take a look at it." He crossed to where Amanda stood and peered over her shoulder as she unfolded the paper. "Well, I'll be damned."

"It's a letter," Amanda said, turning toward Leigh and Freddy. "A letter from Clara. Would one of you like to read it? I'm not a relative or anything."

"Read it," Freddy said. "You're one of the True Love women, now."

Amanda's face lit with pleasure. "Yes, I believe I am."
She turned her attention to the letter. "It says:

> To the person who discovers this gold—On September 19, 1884, Jethro Whitlock and his desperadoes came to my home when Thaddeus was away. They held me at gunpoint while they buried their stolen goods beneath the dirt floor of my home. Jethro will give Thaddeus all the details of my soiled past and implicate Thaddeus and me in the robbery if I tell anyone about the gold. Now that Jethro and his gang has left, I have uncovered the strongbox so that I may insert this note, hoping it will keep suspicion from ever falling on my dear husband. I pray that Jethro retrieves his booty soon and that Thaddeus will never know of its presence in the lovely home he built for me. He risked his reputation to marry a woman of questionable character. I will take this secret to my grave to protect my husband's good name.
>
> In great remorse,
> Clara Singleton

Freddy shook her head in wonder. "To think that the True Love has harbored a fortune for years and none of our ancestors knew it. A treasure was right under Clara's feet all the time."

"That's not where the treasure was, Freddy." Leigh's glance rested on Ry and her sister, then moved on to Chase and Amanda. Finally she crouched next to Joe and laced her fingers through his. "And Clara was smart enough to understand that," she murmured, gazing into the eyes of the man she loved.

# Epilogue

Frederica (Freddy) and Thomas Rycroft (Ry) Mc-
Guinnes named their twin girls Clara, after Freddy's
great-great-great-grandmother Clara Singleton, and
Belinda, after the ranch's loyal cook, Belinda Grimes. Ry
eventually rode Grateful Dead to the buzzer, suffering a
broken rib and a two-day tirade from his wife in the
process.

Amanda and Chase Lavette became parents of a girl they
named Helen Marie, after Chase's mother. Helen turned
out to be a boisterous child who got her older brother
Bart into all sorts of trouble. She was nicknamed "Hel"
by her proud father, who took over most of the child-
rearing duties while Amanda ran an ad agency in Tucson.

Leigh and Joseph (Joe) Gilardini presented Joe's son,
Kyle, with a baby brother. Kyle was allowed to name the
boy, and he chose "Leonard," for his idol Leonard Nimoy. Joe became a successful private investigator largely
due to the information he solicited from his psychic wife.

Kyle Gilardini spent all his Christmas and summer va-
cations at the True Love Ranch and became an accomplished rider who eventually won several junior roping

competitions on his Appaloosa, Spilled Milk. Kyle wrote a research paper for school about the True Love Curse, and discovered that the massacre had actually taken place on Eb Whitlock's property.

Ebenezer (Eb) Whitlock spent many years as a guest of the state of Arizona. He claimed that he was no relation to Jethro Whitlock and had merely found the diary by accident while browsing through Arizona Historical Society files.

The Reward for the recovery of the Butterfield Gold Shipment provided the True Love Ranch with enough revenue to construct a separate house for each of the partners, with enough left over to rebuild the homestead and open it to the public as a museum. Kenny Rogers's documentary about Clara Singleton and the cache of gold she kept hidden under her floor aired on national television.

The True Love Ranch has become a sought-after travel destination for romantics the world over as word spreads that something magic in the desert air inspires true love. Dexter still fetches the mail every day, but he now pushes a cart to handle the slew of wedding invitations and birth announcements that arrive from former guests. With each new expression of joy, the legend grows....

# MOVE OVER, MELROSE PLACE

Come live and love in L.A. with the tenants of Bachelor Arms. Enjoy a year's worth of wonderful love stories and meet colorful neighbors you'll bump into again and again.

From Judith Arnold, bestselling author of over thirty-five novels, comes the conclusion to the legend of Bachelor Arms. Whenever a resident sees "the lady in the mirror," his or her life is changed and no one's more so than Clint McCreary's. Or Hope Henley, who looks exactly like the mysterious woman. Don't miss Judith Arnold's captivating:

**#561 THE LADY IN THE MIRROR** (November 1995)

**#565 TIMELESS LOVE** (December 1995)

Believe the legend...

# HARLEQUIN®
## *Temptation*

'Tis the season...for a little Temptation

**ALL I WANT FOR CHRISTMAS**
by Gina Wilkins #567

**MAN UNDER THE MISTLETOE**
by Debra Carroll #568

Treat yourself to two Christmas gifts—gifts you know you'll want to open early!

Available in December wherever Harlequin books are sold.

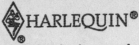
# HARLEQUIN®

Don't miss these Harlequin favorites by some of our most
distinguished authors!
And now you can receive a discount by ordering two or more titles!

| | | |
|---|---|---|
| HT#25593 | WHAT MIGHT HAVE BEEN<br>by Glenda Sanders | $2.99 U.S. ☐ /$3.50 CAN. ☐ |
| HP#11713 | AN UNSUITABLE WIFE<br>by Lindsay Armstrong | $2.99 U.S. ☐ /$3.50 CAN. ☐ |
| HR#03356 | BACHELOR'S FAMILY<br>by Jessica Steele | $2.99 U.S.☐ /$3.50 CAN. ☐ |
| HS#70494 | THE BIG SECRET by Janice Kaiser | $3.39 ☐ |
| HI#22196 | CHILD'S PLAY by Bethany Campbell | $2.89 ☐ |
| HAR#16553 | THE MARRYING TYPE<br>by Judith Arnold | $3.50 U.S. ☐ /$3.99 CAN. ☐ |
| HH#28844 | THE TEMPTING OF JULIA<br>by Maura Seger | $3.99 U.S ☐ /$4.50 CAN. ☐ |

(limited quantities available on certain titles)

| | |
|---|---|
| **AMOUNT** | $ |
| **DEDUCT: 10% DISCOUNT FOR 2+ BOOKS** | $ |
| **POSTAGE & HANDLING** | $ |
| ($1.00 for one book, 50¢ for each additional) | |
| **APPLICABLE TAXES*** | $_____ |
| <u>**TOTAL PAYABLE**</u> | $_____ |
| (check or money order—please do not send cash) | |

To order, complete this form and send it, along with a check or money order for the
total above, payable to Harlequin Books, to: **In the U.S.:** 3010 Walden Avenue,
P.O. Box 9047, Buffalo, NY 14269-9047; **In Canada:** P.O. Box 613, Fort Erie, Ontario,
L2A 5X3.

Name: _____

Address:_____City: _____

State/Prov.: _____Zip/Postal Code: _____

*New York residents remit applicable sales taxes.
 Canadian residents remit applicable GST and provincial taxes.

HBACK-OD2

HARLEQUIN®

*Temptation*

*Secret Fantasies*

*Do you have a secret fantasy?*

Holly Morris does. All she'd ever wanted was to live happily ever after with the man she loved. But a tragic accident shattered that dream. Or had it? Craig Ford strongly reminds her of her former lover. He has the same expressions, the same gestures...and the same memories. Is he her fantasy come to life? Find out in #566, LOOK INTO MY EYES by Glenda Sanders, available in December 1995.

*Everybody* has a secret fantasy. And you'll find them all in Temptation's exciting yearlong miniseries, **Secret Fantasies**. Throughout 1995, one book each month focuses on the hero and heroine's innermost romantic desires....

# A Stetson and spurs don't make a man a cowboy.

Being a real cowboy means being able to tough it out on the ranch and on the range. Three Manhattan city slickers with something to prove meet that challenge...and succeed.

But are they man enough to handle the three wild western women who lasso their hearts?

Bestselling author Vicki Lewis Thompson will take you on the most exciting trail ride of your life with her fabulous new trilogy—**Urban Cowboys.**

**THE TRAILBLAZER** #555 (September 1995)

**THE DRIFTER** #559 (October 1995)

**THE LAWMAN** #563 (November 1995)

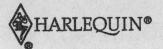

# HARLEQUIN®

# CHRISTMAS ROGUES

## is giving you everything 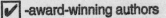 you want on your Christmas list this year:

- ✓ -great romance stories
- ✓ -award-winning authors
- ✓ -a FREE gift promotion
- ✓ -an abundance of Christmas cheer

This November, not only can you join ANITA MILLS, PATRICIA POTTER and MIRANDA JARRETT for exciting, heartwarming Christmas stories about roguish men and the women who tame them—but you can also receive a FREE gold-tone necklace. (Details inside all copies of Christmas Rogues.)

CHRISTMAS ROGUES—romance reading at its best—only from HARLEQUIN BOOKS!

**Available in November wherever Harlequin books are sold.**

HHCR-R

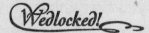